The New Chapter

A Mermaid Cove Romance
Book One

MEGAN JACOBS

Sandy Bay Publishing

Print ISBN: 978-1-0670432-2-3

Ebook ISBN: 978-1-0670432-1-6

Published in New Zealand

First Edition: 2025

The New Chapter

A Mermaid Cove Romance
Book One

A fading marriage. A small-town return. An unexpected second chance.

Esme Gordon never planned to stay in Mermaid Cove longer than a few days until her grandmother's will reveals a surprising twist: a puzzle she must solve to claim her inheritance. It's the first in a series of riddles Grammy left behind, and Esme is the first to take on the challenge.

Her husband Joe isn't thrilled. With his high-pressure job waiting in Chicago, he's ready to leave, and their already fragile marriage is nearing breaking point. But as they work together to unravel Grammy's clues, it stirs buried memories, and Esme questions the life they left behind.

Meanwhile, a wealthy developer with a mysterious past connection to Grammy is quietly trying to buy up local properties, including her beloved beachfront estate. As Esme digs deeper, she realizes the inheritance is about more than a legacy, it's about protecting the heart of the town, and possibly, her own.

With secrets emerging and her marriage on the line, will Esme return to the city life she's built? Or will she fight for a new chapter in the place she never expected to call home?

Welcome to the Mermaid Cove Romance Series – perfect for fans of sweet love stories, surprise twists, small-town charm, and finding yourself where you least expect.

Prologue

THE DOCUMENT IN ESME Gordon's hand was only a few pages long, but as she held it against her chest, it carried the weight of her world.

As her toes sank into the warm sand, Esme strolled along the beach with an overwhelming heaviness in her heart. If the weather dared to match her mood, it would have been stormy, with thunder and lightning. Instead, the evening was as picture-perfect as Southern California could be.

Sunset painted the sky in improbable shades of deep pink, fading to royal purple. The sun shimmered on the watery horizon, a double coin of burnished gold, reflected in the gentle ripple of the waves. With the sea and sky both engulfed in such dramatic color, it was easy to imagine that she had escaped to a different world, somewhere fantastical and worthy of grand adventure.

Esme closed her eyes and tried to picture it, but the importance of the document she held in her hand kept drawing her back to this life, this world that was so bitterly void of magic. Sighing, she stopped and turned her back on the wash of the waves to gaze at the mansion where it towered over its overgrown grounds and the unkempt footpath leading to the beach. The golden evening light bathed its façade in brilliant color, lighting up every window, every roof tile, every streak of peeling paint.

The place seemed sad and empty now. It contained none of the magic that had made Esme's childhood so special despite it all. Perhaps everyone was right... perhaps it was just a house, after all.

Maybe it didn't need to press on Esme's chest like a boulder crushing her ribs.

She knew the thought was ridiculous as soon as it crossed her mind. She clenched her jaw.

She would fight for this place. No matter what.

Chapter One

Two Weeks Earlier

DESPITE THE GENTLE SNORES coming from behind her, Esme Gordon felt as she usually did: alone.

She stared out of the window, peering through the chink between the wall and the elegant ivory white blind. The wall's delicate shade of blue—Shimmer, Esme remembered—complemented the ivory perfectly.

Through the window, though, Esme saw nothing but streaks of rainwater and the blurry gray of the building directly opposite. It did little for the steady ache in her chest.

She rolled onto her back, pulling the comforter up to her chin, and wriggled her toes against sheets of Egyptian cotton with a thread count so high she hadn't known it existed before she moved to Chicago. Beside her, Joe was a tousle of brown hair on his feather pillow, his back to her. Her husband had been asleep for—Esme checked—eleven hours. Poor soul.

Rolling over, she wrapped her arm gently around him and pressed her face against the smooth skin of his back. He smelled delicious at this time in the morning, before he could coat himself with expensive cologne. He smelled indescribably of *Joe*, an absolutely unique fragrance, the most heavenly thing in the world.

She closed her eyes tight, inhaling his scent, and wished he'd wake up. She'd been tossing and turning beside him for the past three hours.

Instead, Joe just sighed and slept on, and Esme gave up. She tucked the comforter tightly around him, rolled out of bed and padded on bare feet to the kitchen. Its sleek surfaces of granite and metal, utterly pristine, and the broad window overlooking the bustling street all pleased the interior designer that Esme really was. It was perfect. She knew because this kitchen had been her first project, fresh out of college, when she'd loaded everything into her little hatchback and driven across the country in desperation to get started on her career.

That had been five years ago. She'd known the moment she stepped through those doors and saw the apartment—then shabby—and the suave, smiling young man who awaited her that she was in love.

She ran her fingers over the smooth countertop as she switched on the electric kettle. It was perfect, all right. A triumph of interior design. She used pictures of this kitchen for her website. Joe had only told her much later that it was her headshot on her website that had enticed him to hire an unknown, wet-behind-the-ears designer even though he could have afforded someone established.

With the coffee brewing, Esme grabbed the non-stick pan from the cabinet and turned on an element. She tossed bread in the toaster and started on a batch of scrambled eggs. The movements felt mechanical, almost pointless. The sputter of the eggs in the pan could do little to dispel the silence that always hung in this kitchen. In this house.

Don't be absurd, Esme told herself. *Joe's right here.* She couldn't help wondering for how long.

Finally, Joe shuffled into the kitchen just as Esme was buttering the toast, too endearing for words in his rumpled shorts and messy hair. He didn't say anything, just leaned on Esme from behind and wrapped his arms around her waist.

"Hey, honey." Esme tilted her head back.

"Hi, beautiful." Joe's lips tickled her neck as he spoke.

"You sleep well?"

"Mmm. Feels like I'm still sleeping well. Smells nice in here."

"Doesn't it?" Esme turned and wrapped her arms around him, relishing his warmth, his nearness as they held each other. "Do you want bacon, too?"

"I want *you*." Joe playfully tickled her ribs.

Esme squealed and slapped his hands away, laughing. "Focus, baby! Bacon or no bacon?"

Joe's rakish grin lit up his hazel eyes. "Bacon would be great. You sit. I've got this."

Esme perched at the kitchen island, sipping her coffee while Joe hunted in the fridge for the bacon. The muscles in his back rippled as he peered through the shelves and eventually fished it out. The smell of it sizzling soon filled the kitchen.

She wrapped her hands around her coffee mug, watching. Something like desperation filled her. If only these moments could last longer between them.

"How did the movie end last night?" Joe asked, grabbing his own cup of coffee.

"The hero got the girl, but not the treasure. Grammy would disapprove."

"She prefers treasure to girls?"

"Not exactly." Esme laughed. "She's always saying that the hero can have both, if he really is a hero."

Joe chuckled. "Considering that your grammy owns half of California thanks to her books, I'm not going to argue with that."

"Half of California." Esme scoffed. "You're exaggerating."

"We'll just stick with that story around my parents." Joe said it as a joke, but Esme shifted her weight uncomfortably, aware that her trust-fund-baby husband had parents who weren't exactly thrilled about his marrying some penniless kid out of college, not even if that kid had a millionaire for a grandmother.

Joe nudged the bacon with a spatula and frowned. “Sorry, honey. I didn’t mean it like that.”

“Don’t worry. I understand you don’t. You’re home all day today, right?”

Joe’s shoulders stiffened. “Yes, Esme. That’s what I said, remember?”

Esme looked away, stung by his sharp tone.

“I’ll be here all day,” Joe added, more gently this time.

Esme managed a tight-lipped smile. “So, what do you want to do today? Go to the mall? Stay in bed and watch movies?” *It’s been a long time since we had a whole Saturday to ourselves,* she added silently. “I’ll pick a more interesting movie this time.”

“Aw, honey, the movie was great. I’m sorry.” Joe served the perfectly cooked bacon. “I was just really tired last night.”

“I’m not surprised,” said Esme gently. “You worked overtime every day last week.”

“I know. You know how it is. It’s that time of year.”

Esme said nothing. It seemed to her that it was always *that time of year* at the accounting firm where Joe worked.

"Let's stay at home," Joe suggested, sitting opposite her and pushing her plate over to her. "I'm exhausted."

"Okay, babe. That sounds like a great idea." Esme tried to hide a swift pang of disappointment. She would have loved to head to the mall and get out amongst people. She'd spent the entire week sitting here at home, marketing her skills, improving her website, and checking her emails ten thousand times an hour to see if her last client had sent a renewed contract yet. Maybe they never would, and then what would she do with herself?

Joe tucked into his eggs. "Maybe we can watch the end of the movie again now."

"Sure," said Esme. They always did. Friday nights were supposed to be movie nights, but Joe was so tired and got home so late that he seldom made it more than thirty minutes in.

"We could make waffles for lunch," Joe said. "They're quick and easy, and we can walk to the corner store for whipped cream."

"Oh, yes. What about—"

Joe's phone rang deafeningly on the corner of the island. They both tensed.

"It's the office."

Esme didn't say anything, but turned back to her breakfast, spearing a piece of toast with a sharp jab of her fork.

Joe grimaced. "Sorry. I'll be quick." He dropped his fork, grabbed the phone and went to the bedroom, answering it cheerfully with, "Hi, Mike. How can I help you?"

"'How can I help you?'" Esme grumbled. "What about, 'What do you want? I'm spending a weekend with my wife for once'?" She got up and put Joe's plate into the microwave to keep it warm. She knew he'd be a while.

Esme had finished eating when Joe came back into the kitchen, and she instantly recognized the look in his eyes. Her shoulders sagged. "Don't tell me..."

"I'm so sorry, baby. They need me urgently. There's an issue with that major company's audit and they're not going to manage without me." Joe grabbed his toast out of the microwave, leaving the rest of his breakfast on the plate. "I'll be back soon, I'm sure."

"Heard that before," Esme said under her breath.

Joe stared at her. "What do you want from me? This is my job we're talking about. The job that pays for everything."

"Excuse me?" Esme's head snapped up.

Joe gritted his teeth. "I didn't mean it like that. Of course your work is important, too."

"Not more important than you are," Esme blurted out.

Joe stared at her. "That's not fair. You can't act like I'm a bad husband because I work hard."

"That's not what I mean," Esme said, staring at her empty plate.

"What would you have me do? Tell the office that I'm not coming in because my wife doesn't like it?"

All I want is for you to stay here for once, Esme mused, but arguing would achieve nothing.

"I won't be gone all day. Call a friend. Go shopping or something. I'll be home before you know it."

Joe was dressed and ready before she was done rinsing the dishes. He gave her a peck on the cheek, car keys jingling, and disappeared before she could say 'I love you'.

She mumbled the words anyway, staring at the closed door, and let out a heavy sigh as she slumped into her chair at the kitchen island. It was raining harder now; the drops drummed against the window, and a low gray mist hung over the street. Cars swished past, regardless, their headlights pale in the rain. The apartment felt colder than ever.

Chapter Two

Call a friend, Joe had said. Anything would be better than sitting here in the stony silence of this beautiful, empty apartment. Briefly, Esme imagined piling into bed with a heap of happy children and pushed the thought away. She pulled out her phone instead and scrolled through her recent contacts.

Her eye caught on a name on her phone. *Grammy Hamilton.* Esme hesitated, then tapped the video call button. If she was sitting here losing her mind, then Grammy was the only person who could help her find it again.

The phone rang repeatedly, and just as Esme was about to give up, it connected. The screen showed a shaky, blurry video of a double chin and some nostrils.

"Grammy?"

"Esme, my little fairy godmother," Grammy trilled, giving Esme an excellent view of her false teeth. The phone went to her ear, giving Esme an uncomfortably close view of wiry ear hair she could never unsee.

"Grammy, look at the phone. It's a video call. You're showing me your ear."

"Oh, lovely. Then you'll see my newest earrings." Grammy moved the phone, and Esme finally looked into her grandmother's creased, smiling face. Grammy had comfortable, squishy proportions, sparkling blue eyes, and a wild mop of gray curls that she was always dyeing in weird colors. Today's variation was streaks of shocking pink and bright blue.

"Hey, Grammy." Esme laughed. "Love the hair."

"Thank you, fairy. Yours looks fabulous, too. Definitely love the bird's nest look. Very elven of you."

Esme peered at her reflection in the bottom corner of the screen. "Yikes. Sorry. I guess I've still got some bedhead going on." She attempted to subdue her rebellious bob.

Grammy burst into laughter. "No worries, darling. So, how's it going in cold, gray, smelly Chicago?"

"Cold, gray, and smelly."

"No surprises there."

"How about sunny Mermaid Cove?" Esme asked. "How's everything there?"

"Oh, lovely as usual, fairy. Perfect weather, gorgeous ocean. We had the biggest thunderstorm the other night. It shook the walls and windows like a dragon prowling the estate. I opened a window and stood in the rain."

"Grammy!"

"A cold, bracing rainstorm is good for the spirits."

Esme laughed. "Aren't you afraid of lightning?"

"I love rain more than I fear lightning."

"Quoting your own books today, are we?"

"Possibly. Why not?" Grammy's eyes sparkled. "Oh, you'll like this. We had a little drama in the village last week."

"What happened?" said Esme.

"You remember wonderful Julio, the one who has the fishing boat that brings all the lovely fresh fish to stores and restaurants in the village?"

Esme nodded. "I've waved to him a few times. He always used to deliver right to your house. Didn't you help him buy a fishing boat after his parents died in that tragedy at sea?"

Grammy didn't speak of her charity often and today was no exception. "He still does, darling. Nothing as wonderful as a nice bream in the frying pan that was alive two hours ago. He's such a nice young man. I wonder if he and Louise still talk."

"I don't think Louise talks to anyone much," said Esme.

"You're right there, sweetie. And she thinks I'm the introvert. Anyway, so dear old Preston thought he could buy out Julio's business. Boat, boathouse, client list and all."

"Preston?"

"Preston Langford, honey," Grammy explained.

"Is that the real estate mogul from San Diego? I've seen his ads—they always pop up on Facebook after I've visited Mermaid Cove. Doesn't he buy up land to develop into huge complexes?"

"Sure does, sweetie. He's been trying to buy parts of Mermaid Cove for years. He'd like nothing more than to pollute our coastline with fancy hotels." Anger was palpable in Grammy's voice.

"Is he building a hotel near you?" Esme asked, dismayed.

"Oh, no, dearie. I wouldn't let that happen." Grammy chuckled. "The people who live here and own land here truly love this place. If they ever consider selling to Preston, it's because they need something. And when I find out they need something, well, I help them out."

"You do?"

"Yes, of course. Where do you think the bookstore came from, fairy? Preston wanted to turn that cute little place into an apartment building, so I bought it and gave it to my dear friend Corrie. Anyway, he tried to buy Julio's boat knowing that the catch wasn't good this year, so Julio came to me. Tried to sell me the boat back. Absurd, really," said Grammy breezily. "I took care of it, and of course, Preston was furious. You should see the emails I've been getting."

"Took care of it?"

"Oh, you know. I sorted it out. Nothing to it. So Preston sent me the most ridiculous emails." Grammy burst out laughing. "You'd swear he was trying to intimidate me. He really should know better."

"I'm sorry, Grammy. That sounds rough."

"Not at all, dear. I've handled book reviewers for decades. I think I can handle foolish old Preston Langford. Enough about Mermaid Cove now. Tell me about you. How are you, fairy?"

As much as Esme longed to unburden her heart, instead she asked, "How's the book?"

"Coming on, dear. I've planned out the ending at last. Now I just need to get there." Grammy smiled. "It's always my favorite part, you know. It's the part where it all comes together."

"As if you've ever really written an ending," Esme teased. "How many books are there in the *Tales of Otherworld* series now? Twenty-one?"

"Twenty-two, when this one is finished," Grammy confirmed. "Besides, why would you put an end to something wonderful if you didn't have to?"

"Joe would say that it would be ridiculous to end something that's making as much money as your series does."

Grammy laughed. "Oh, fairy, that sounds like Joe, but it's never been about money. You know that."

"I know. I think that's why they sell so well, Grammy. They're so filled with hope and joy. Not many books are, these days."

"Listen to you. These days. As if you're the grandma around here." Grammy's smile faded. "Honestly, fairy, with the amount of frown lines you've got going on, perhaps people are going to start mistaking you for me."

"Grammy," Esme protested.

"I'm joking, Esme. Well, I'm joking about the frown lines. You do look like you've been frowning lately, though. What's the matter, little fairy?"

Esme sighed. "I didn't phone you just to rant."

"I know you didn't. You had to get a glimpse of my beautiful face." Grammy plumped up her wild hair.

Esme couldn't help but laugh.

"I can see something's bothering you, fairy. Tell me what it is." Grammy sat down with a grunt in her favorite armchair; Esme recognized the swirling pink and gold patterns of the upholstery behind her. "I'm here to help."

"Thanks, Grammy. Sometimes it feels like I have no one else to talk to. Mom can be sort of judgmental sometimes."

Grammy groaned.

"Dad... it's like he just does what Mom wants. Margot and Louise are so far away. And Isabel...well." Esme cleared her throat.

"We don't talk about Isabel," Grammy sang.

"Grammy, you know it's more complicated than that."

"It seldom really is, fairy, but why don't you talk to Joe, then?"

The question brought Esme up short. Tears pricked her eyes.

"Oh, my darling, what's wrong?"

"Nothing, really." Esme wiped her eyes. "Joe is wonderful, Grammy. I've never felt so loved in my whole life. I know he cares about me, and when we're together, everything just seems amazing."

"When you're together?"

"Yeah." Esme sighed. "He's always at work. He's at work right now, actually. I know he wants to do well for us—not that I don't have work of my own—but it's not as though we're struggling for money." She swung her legs, glancing around the kitchen filled with shiny appliances. "I don't know how to make him understand that I don't want more stuff. I just want him."

"It could be as simple as that," said Grammy. "As simple as just saying it."

Esme raised an eyebrow. "That seems too simple."

"It worked for Rod and me, sweetie." Grammy's eyes filled with sorrow and love. "Worked for many, many years."

"I think your marriage worked just because you and Grandpa were the two coolest people I've ever known."

Grammy burst out laughing. "Oh, fairy, if you only knew the half of it. When are all of you coming down for a little vacation in Mermaid Cove, anyway? It's been ages."

"I know. Joe said maybe this summer. I don't know about anyone else."

"I think it would do you good, fairy."

"You must be so lonely down there."

Grammy hooted. "Lonely? Lonely! Oh, you are funny. I have the sea and the gulls and all of my stories to keep me company." Her eyes shone. "Don't you worry, Esme. Grammy's doing just fine here."

Esme leaned back in her seat and smiled. "That's good to hear, Grammy."

"It's you lot that I worry about. Scattered all across the continent. Wait, that's a good line. Where's my notebook?"

Esme laughed. "So, what's the next adventure for Tardin of Merrabor?"

Grammy's eyes gleamed. "Oh, fairy, you'll love it."

She launched into an excited explanation of the plot for her next book, and Esme took the phone to her bedroom, curled up on the huge empty bed, and listened.

A buzzing near her head woke Esme so early on Sunday morning that the dawn light was still gray and feeble behind the curtains. She groaned, dismayed. Joe had only gotten home at four o'clock yesterday, and now the office was summoning him again, leaving them no time even for breakfast together.

She curled up on her side, pulling the sheets up to her chin, pretending to be asleep just so that Joe would have to wrap his arms around her to wake her and tell her that he was leaving. She felt him stirring, turning over and fumbling on his nightstand for the phone, but the buzzing continued.

"Essie?" Joe sat up. "Es, your phone's ringing."

Esme's eyes snapped open. The phone was lit up on her nightstand, still buzzing, and the name on the screen was *Mom*.

"What?" Esme mumbled.

"It's your mom, baby." Joe rubbed her shoulder. "You'd better answer."

It was seven in the morning, and a sudden, cold fear spread through Esme's gut. She scrambled to grab the phone and held it to her ear. "Mom?"

She hadn't heard her mother's voice in three weeks, and she couldn't say that she'd missed it when Gwen Hamilton's nasal tones grated through the phone lines. "Esme, thank goodness. I thought you'd never pick up. Are you still sleeping with your phone on silent?"

Esme sagged into the pillows, rubbing her eyes. "Hey, Mom."

"You really shouldn't," Gwen chided. "You never know when someone will urgently need to speak to you."

Esme stifled a yawn. "It's seven in the morning, Mom. Is everything okay?"

The long, long silence made Esme's heart freeze in her chest. She sat up, suddenly wide awake.

"Mom." Esme swallowed. "Tell me everything's okay."

"I'm sorry." Gwen's voice was cold and calm. "Grammy has died."

The words slammed into Esme's chest like a sledgehammer. She clutched her heart, which felt like it had stopped, so she couldn't understand the wild fluttering she felt beneath her fingers. "What?"

Joe stared at her, wide-eyed.

"She passed away in her sleep last night," said Gwen. "The handyman found her this morning."

"But she couldn't have," Esme said in disbelief. "I spoke to her yesterday."

"Yes, well, she did, Esme."

Tears stung Esme's eyes. Why hadn't they gone to visit Grammy last summer? Why had they left it so long?

How could this have happened?

"What...how?" Esme sobbed. "How did this happen?"

"She was old, Esme," said Gwen. "Her heart gave out, it seems. They say it was peaceful."

Peaceful? It was death. Esme couldn't understand how it could have happened so quickly. Tears overwhelmed her, coursing down her cheeks as she clasped a hand over her mouth, trying to hold them back.

Gwen was saying something.

"Did you hear me?" she asked.

"N-no," Esme stammered. "What was that?"

"I said that we'll all have to go down to that hateful house now. For the funeral and the will reading. Next week. Can you be there?"

"Of course," Esme managed. "I don't—I'll let you know." She pinched the bridge of her nose and tried to regain control over her breathing.

"Okay. You do that." Gwen hesitated. "Esme, I'm sorry."

"M,,,Mom?" Esme said gently.

"Yes?"

"She was your mom." Esme swallowed. "I'm sorry. This must be awful for you."

There was a long silence. Gwen cleared her throat painfully, like she was holding back an emotion that she never let Esme or her siblings see.

"Let me know," she said again, and hung up.

The phone tumbled from Esme's numb fingers. Joe was staring at her, his hand resting on her knee, concern creasing the skin between his eyebrows.

Esme took deep breaths, struggling to stay calm. She reached for her phone again, the movement automatic. She knew exactly who to call. Someone who would instantly make her feel better, whose wisdom would carry her through this difficulty.

Grammy.

She covered her face with her hands, a moan of agony escaping her as realization made her feel like she'd fallen over the edge of a cliff.

Grammy was dead.

Chapter Three

No matter how many times Esme saw this piece of coastline, it would always take her breath away.

The ocean glimmered underneath her as the plane made a wide turn over the water, aquamarine and turquoise, every conceivable shade of blue. It foamed white against a strip of shining golden beach, dotted with colorful swimmers and surfers, umbrellas and beach blankets, cars shimmering in the parking lot near the sand.

"Look at it, Joe, we're here," Esme said.

She squinted to the horizon, wondering like she always did if she could actually see Mermaid Cove from here. The tiny town would be little more than a speck against the sand. Instead, the plane turned toward the city of Santa Maria and began its descent.

"Joe?" Esme turned.

Joe was hunched over his laptop, chewing his lip as he typed something into a spreadsheet. Esme didn't think he'd looked up a single time since they'd boarded the plane. He'd held her hand loosely in the airport, his phone permanently clamped to his ear, leaving Esme to sort out boarding passes and luggage.

"Joe, honey." Esme bit back her annoyance and nudged him with her knee.

"Mm, what?" he grunted.

"We're here. We're landing. You need to put away your laptop."

Joe flashed her an annoyed look, then closed the laptop and slid it into his case. He checked his watch. "We're late."

"We were delayed in Chicago, remember?"

"Mmm-hmm." Joe sighed. "Don't I just."

Esme flinched. "What's that supposed to mean?"

He stared at her, then shook his head. "Nothing. Nothing. Sorry, honey. Nothing."

They sat in silence as the plane bumped down on the runway.

"Do you want to get something to eat here, or shall we drive to Mermaid Cove first?" Esme asked. "We've had nothing since breakfast, but I think Mom and Dad are already at the house. Maybe we should get there so that they're not sitting there all alone."

"We'll eat at the airport. I need to send some emails before we start the drive."

Esme stared at him. "More emails? I thought you said you'd have time off for this, babe."

"Yeah, well, so did I," said Joe, "but the customer is always right, and the customer wants the data right away."

Esme's toes curled. She couldn't remember when last she'd slept a full night. Certainly not since the news about Grammy. Exhaustion and sorrow created annoyance in her chest.

"Is this how it's going to be the whole time we're here?" she demanded.

Joe stared at her. "What do you mean?"

"You haven't looked up from your phone or laptop since we left the house this morning. Are you going to be able to put your phone down for the funeral?"

"What are you talking about?" Joe snapped. "Of course I'm going to be able to put it down for the funeral. You're being unreasonable, Esme. Stop it."

Esme looked away, a hole torn in her heart. She couldn't understand why he had to hurt her when she was already broken.

"I don't have a choice," said Joe sharply. "If I'm going to get this promotion, I have to go all out."

"Yes, I know."

And after that? she wanted to ask him. *Will you be happy with the next promotion, or the next, or the next?* But her heart felt too heavy for her to squeeze out another word.

The dress code on the invitation to Grammy's funeral was to wear white.

Esme's summer dress swirled around her legs in the sea breeze as she struggled across the beach, her wedges wobbling in the warm golden sand. It was the kind of day that Grammy would have called an 'outside writing day'; a day so perfect that the old lady would have taken her trusty laptop down to the beach or outside to the garden to work. How many times had Esme watched her, hunched over a folding tray, her fingers flying across the keys, lips pursed in concentration? She'd always thought Grammy looked comical as she worked. That was before she'd known that her grandmother was capable of making magic.

She shook her head, trying to dispel the memory, as Joe's hand tightened over hers. Their fingers were both slippery and sweaty. "You okay, babe?"

Esme couldn't look at him. At least he'd finally put away his phone.

"Fine."

Joe raised his eyebrows as they continued along the beach. "Looks more like a wedding than a funeral."

He was right. The white folding chairs were stacked along the sand and wrapped in lightweight white fabric that stirred in the breeze like sea foam. Flower petals, pink and purple, were scattered over the chairs and giant frangipani blooms hung in glass bottles at the end of each row of chairs. The driftwood lectern at the front of the seating was wrapped in jasmine, and a cheerful old pastor leaned on it, smiling faintly.

Esme's heart flipped in her chest. The small table in front of the lectern sported a white tablecloth, a vase of flowers, a photograph, and an urn. The photograph was Grammy's author photo, the one she loved, standing barefoot in the waves and wearing a loudly colorful bikini designed for someone significantly younger. Her wild hair streamed around her head in the wind, and her smile was radiant, even immortalized behind glass.

The urn looked far too small to contain someone so unequaled.

Esme brushed tears from her cheeks as they shuffled up to the seating. A speaker near the lectern played "I Can Only Imagine", which made her cry more.

"You okay?" Joe asked again.

"Fine," she said again.

The seats were mostly full. Esme glanced over them, recognizing a handful of people from the tourist village of Mermaid Cove. Her sisters, Margot and Louise, sat huddled close together near the front. Her mom and dad, Gwen Hamilton and Lance Weston, sat at the other end of the row from the two girls. Lance's face was a granite mask. Gwen sat up very straight and still, dry-eyed, her hands folded in her lap.

"You're late," Gwen accused as Joe and Esme scooted past her.

"Plane was delayed," Esme mumbled.

She could still feel her mother's eyes stabbing into her back as she moved into a seat next to her sisters.

Margot was the first to stretch out her hands to Esme. Her face was scarlet, tears streaming down her cheeks in a streaky mess of makeup, and her hands trembled when she clutched Esme's. "Oh, Essie."

"I know." Esme tried to swallow the lump in her throat. "I know."

Louise dabbed at her eyes with a tissue. They were red and puffy, but her voice quivered with control. "It was so quick."

"I think..." Esme cleared her throat. "I think Grammy would have wanted it that way."

Louise looked at the urn. "Yes, I guess you're right."

A car's engine rumbled, and Esme glanced up as a gleaming silver Rolls-Royce Phantom stopped at the funeral's edge. A tall, thin gray haired man stepped out and strode down the aisle purposefully, swinging a walking stick. Esme felt sorry for him that he was late, too.

Margot wrapped her arms around Esme, and she leaned into her sister's hug. Joe nodded a greeting to both girls.

"Has anyone seen Isabel?" Esme asked, pulling back from the embrace.

Louise scoffed and looked away.

"I'm sure she's coming," said Margot firmly. "Maybe her plane got delayed, too."

Isabel hadn't come to Esme's wedding ceremony, but she didn't say that, not now. Not to Margot.

Joe wrapped her hand in his own as the music stopped and the pastor stepped forward.

"Dear friends," he said, his voice soft over the rumble of the surf, "welcome to the celebration of the life of Alicia Hamilton, a treasured mother, friend, and grandmother to so many."

Esme's lower lip trembled, and Joe squeezed her hand harder.

"I know she leaves a great hole in our lives. Sunday mornings will be hard without her face in the pew." The pastor's eyes shone with emotion beneath an explosive mop of red curls. "I believe that all of you—excuse me, sir, can I help you?"

The old man who'd come from the Rolls-Royce stood in front of the lectern, staring at the picture of Grammy. His back was very straight although he leaned on his walking stick with both hands.

"Sir?" the pastor prompted.

"I didn't get an invitation," said the old man.

Everyone stared at him.

"I saw the funeral details on the bookstore's Facebook page," said the old man, his voice still soft. "But nobody bothered to invite me."

"Who is this guy?" Margot whispered.

"I don't know," said Louise, "but he seems familiar."

Esme nodded. "He does. He seems confused, poor guy."

"We're glad that you're here with us now, sir," said the pastor. "Why don't you take a seat, and—"

"Oh, Alicia." The old man sighed heavily and reached out to trace his fingertips over the picture. "Now we'll never have our chance. How could you do this to me? How could you push me away even now?"

"Sir," said the pastor, "I think you should—"

"You don't understand." The old man's voice filled with sudden rage. "You don't know what she did to me, and all I ever did was love her."

Esme exchanged a glance with her sisters, who shrugged. In the front row, Gwen rolled her eyes.

"Sir, please take your seat," said the pastor firmly.

The old man turned, and Esme saw his face clearly for the first time. She recognized him suddenly from his social media ads.

"That's Preston," she hissed.

"Who?" Margot asked.

"Preston Langford," Esme explained. "A real estate developer. He's been trying to buy up Mermaid Cove."

"Seems like he and Grammy had a history," said Louise.

"None of you know what she did to me," Preston cried shaking his stick. "Even now, you keep me away."

"Sir." Esme's father, Lance, rose to his feet. "You're disturbing her funeral. Please, have some respect."

"All I wanted was to love her, and she pushed me away," Preston seethed.

Lance took his arm. "Please sit down, sir."

Preston shook off his grasp and cast a last, sneering glance over the funeral. He had the palest blue eyes Esme had ever seen and an aquiline nose that must have made him handsome, once, but deep wrinkles had marred the smooth lines of his face.

"No. It's all right," he snapped. "I'm leaving anyway."

He spun around and stalked back to the Rolls, stick under his arm. The guests murmured and nudged each other, confused.

"What was he talking about?" Louise asked. "What did Grammy do to him?"

"Nothing," said Margot fiercely. "Grammy never did anything to anyone."

Esme shook her head. "He must be confused. Maybe he has dementia or something." She couldn't imagine Grammy hurting anyone, either.

"Sorry about that, folks," said the pastor, silencing the crowd. The Rolls roared as he drove away. "Let's get back to celebrating our friend Alicia, shall we?"

The crowd gave a murmur of assent. To his credit, the pastor smoothly slipped back into the service.

"Alicia didn't leave behind many instructions for her funeral," he went on. "That's not to say she never thought of her own mortality. Friends, the number of times Alicia would tell me that she couldn't wait to see Heaven is shocking. She loved this life more than anyone I've ever known, but she also knew that something far better was waiting for her. She couldn't wait to go into the arms of her Savior. I know your grief is great, and it should be for a woman like her. But it is not Alicia who is grieving anymore."

Esme couldn't help smiling through her tears. The knowledge that her grandmother was safe at last was the only comfort she could find in her heart.

"Before we begin with the service, Alicia's best friend, Corrie Doornvlei, would like to read an excerpt from one of Alicia's own books." The pastor stepped back.

An old lady shuffled painfully to the lectern. She was comfortably round, from the hips clad in a floral dress to the perfect curves of her silver bob, and her blue eyes welling as she took her place. Her copy of the seventh volume of *Tales of Otherworld* was worn and creased.

Corrie cleared her throat and read, her voice gaining strength as the words flowed.

"*'Oh, my young friend,' the magician said, 'why are you so afraid to die?'*"

Tears spilled from Esme's eyes. The line was one of her favorites because it had been one of Grammy's favorites.

"*'How could I not be afraid?' Tardin replied,*" Corrie went on. "*'It's death.'*

"*'Has it never occurred to you,' said the magician, 'that death is merely the gateway to something better?'*

"*Tardin looked up at the burning mountainside, ringed with scarlet as the dragon sun rose.*

"*'If we have nothing to fear from death,' the magician said softly, 'then we have nothing to fear.'*

"*Tardin lifted her broadsword. 'Then* I *have nothing to fear,' she said, and went on to meet the dragon.*"

Corrie took a few deep breaths to compose herself. Joe squeezed Esme tightly, and she now sobbed openly.

"Alicia never wrote anything she didn't believe in," said Corrie. "She lived the way she died: absolutely fearless. She was a little old lady who wrote books, but to me, she was a greater hero than any of her armored knights."

Esme covered her face with her hands as the service went on. She was only able to stop her tears when the pastor handed Gwen the urn with Grammy's ashes and gestured to the beach. Lance, Margot, Esme, and Louise followed Gwen to the edge of the water.

Gwen stared at the urn for a long time, but didn't open it.

Esme swallowed and stepped forward. "Mom, do you want—"

"Yes." Gwen thrust the urn into Esme's hands.

Esme unstoppered it, and the ashes blew around in the breeze, fine and gray. It was difficult to imagine that they had anything to do with the vibrant woman that Esme had spoken to on the phone just a few days ago. She stretched out her arms and shook the urn, and the ashes floated out on the breeze and settled on the surface of the water, where wave after little wave swallowed them and washed them out to sea.

Chapter Four

THE CAFÉ SMELLED OF battered fish and garlic butter. Ordinarily, Esme's mouth watered just passing by it on the street, but now she found herself staring into her glass of lemon water with no appetite.

The charming little place was close enough to the beach that fine grains of sand were scattered over the hardwood floor, which had seen better days. Diners sat at wooden tables, all painted different shades of blue-green. A decal of swimming fish played across one wall; the other was a glass sliding door, currently wide open to allow the soft breeze coming in over the beach only a few yards away.

Hungry surfers, sunburned families and crotchety old fishermen alike traded stories, made vacation plans and stuffed their faces with fresh-caught seafood. Only Esme's family was a pool of silence, picking sparsely at the rich platter of prawns, mussels and calamari in the center of the table.

Gwen's hand trembled slightly as she sipped her iced tea. "Come on, everyone." She nudged the platter. "It wasn't cheap, you know. Don't let it go to waste."

"Mom, why are you talking about money at a time like this?" Margot snapped.

"Easy, Margie, easy." Lance extended a hand toward her. "There's no need to be like that."

Margot's eyes welled. "I'm sorry, Dad. I just...I...I miss her so much," she wailed, and burst into tears.

Margot's outburst made Esme want to cry. She blinked rapidly, noticed that Gwen was still glaring, and dutifully popped a mussel into her mouth. It felt like sand on her tongue, but she ate it anyway.

"Who was that man at the funeral, anyway?" Margot choked out.

"Preston Langford," said Gwen. "The real estate guy. He and your grandmother knew each other when they were young."

Esme raised her head in surprise. Gwen seldom ever talked about Grammy. "They did? How?"

"I don't know, and neither do I care," Gwen snapped.

At the rising tension, Louise wiped her eyes, lifted her plate and scooped up sensible little portions of everything. "So, Joe, how's work?"

Joe lit up in a way that made Esme's heart sting. "Really good, thank you. We just went through a major audit with flying colors."

"I've also got an audit coming up, but I'm confident I'll do well," said Louise, smiling.

"Of course you will, honey," said Gwen, her features relaxing. "You've been a superstar with your freelancing ever since you started. I had my doubts about the digital nomad thing, but now I can see that it really was the road to success for you."

Louise looked away. "Thanks, Mom," she mumbled.

Esme didn't know how they could talk about auditors and freelancing when she'd just scattered her grandmother's ashes. The mussel felt like it was going to make a comeback, so she slurped lemon water.

"Grammy wouldn't want us to be sad." Margot wiped her eyes on her sleeve and held Lance's hand tightly. "You guys know that, right? She'd want us to eat this great food and then enjoy our time here."

Lance nodded. "That's right, darling. She would."

Esme smiled. "I can't argue with that."

"Me neither." Louise laughed. "Grammy was always so happy. Being around her was like getting a shot of happiness."

"That's true," said Joe. "She had a knack for putting people in a good mood."

"I think she would have loved her funeral," said Esme. "It was so pretty."

"Ridiculous if you ask me," Gwen grunted. "Whatever happened to funerals being solemn affairs?"

"We'll be sure to make yours as depressing as possible someday, Mom," said Margot sharply.

"Margot," Lance scolded.

"Do you know what Grammy would really have wanted at this funeral, Mom?" said Margot.

"Don't start," Gwen warned.

"Margie." Louise put a hand on her sister's shoulder. "Easy."

"She would have wanted Isabel to be there," said Margot.

"Isabel made her choices." Gwen slurped her iced tea.

"You were the one who chased her away," Margot burst out.

"Margot, that's enough." Lance's voice slammed like a door.

Margot glowered at him and snatched her hand away. "I'm going for a walk." She shoved back her chair and strode out of the café.

"Margot!" Lance yelled.

Everyone in the café stared as Margot stormed out and disappeared onto the beach.

Joe shifted in his chair and cleared his throat uncomfortably. Esme's toes curled, and she buried her face in her lemon water, wishing she was anywhere but here with this family that had been messy enough before it lost the grandmother who'd been its beating heart.

Chapter Five

ESME HAD ALWAYS THOUGHT of Grammy's study as the place where magic was born.

Grammy used to tell her that magic came from inside, not from the place you were sitting when you wrote. Esme smiled fondly as she strolled through the massive room, remembering Grammy's stories of the places where the first books of her series had been written: a kitchenette of the tiny flat where she'd raised Gwen, the back office of the restaurant she'd managed in San Diego before the third book finally took off and became a New York Times bestseller, sitting in the car in the school pickup line.

It was only after the series had become a resounding success, of course, that Grammy had been able to buy the mansion in Mermaid Cove.

There was no part of the house that Esme didn't love, but the study was her favorite. It was part Victorian library, part beach house. The study protruded from the side of the house like a giant bay window, a massive, hexagonal room. Three of its sides were glass doors that could be pushed open to allow the ocean breeze in.

The beach was so close that sand sometimes blew in onto the polished hardwood floor. The other three walls were floor-to-ceiling bookshelves, and it all rose to meet a domed ceiling that Grammy's artist friend had painted in scenes from her books. Knights and dragons, unicorns and fairies chased each other in blues and purples and splashes of brilliant white and gold across the ceiling. A crystal chandelier hung from the center, and there were lamps everywhere. In the evening, they bathed the room in warm light.

Grammy's laptop was even still there on the mahogany desk that faced the sea. She always had the newest laptop, and her fingers worked so fast that she went through keyboards the way most people went through shoes. There were stacks of beautiful leather-bound notebooks, too. Esme trailed her fingers over the back of one.

Soft footsteps behind her made her turn around. Joe stood in the doorway, watching her.

"Hey." Esme smiled. "I didn't see you there."

She watched his face closely. He'd hardly spoken a word to her last night after the spat at Footprints in the Sand over dinner. She wasn't sure that his Zoom call for half the evening had been the only reason.

Joe glanced at his watch. "What time did the lawyer say he'd be here?"

"Nine," said Esme.

Joe nodded. "Any minute now, I guess."

The giant grandfather clock in one corner showed it was five to midnight. Its pendulum swung back and forth, the rhythmic tick filling the room like a heartbeat.

Esme sagged into one of the comfortably squashy couches that faced the desk. "You know, I was almost scared to come into this study this morning," she said. "I always loved it here, but I thought it would be different with Grammy gone."

Joe's face softened. He put his phone into his pocket and sat down beside her, draping an arm around her shoulders. "Is it?"

"Well… it would be impossible for it to be exactly the same, I guess. But it's still magical in its way."

Joe tipped back his head and smiled at the ceiling. "This place really is beautiful." He gazed at the ocean through the closed doors, rippling and perfect as the morning light danced on its surface. "What a fantastic place to live. Maybe we can retire to a place like this someday."

Esme leaned her head against his shoulder. "That's the dream, right?"

"Yeah." Joe kissed her forehead. "That's the dream."

Voices came down the hallway toward them. Margot and Louise crashed into the study, heads close together.

"… believe that Mom's still being so stubborn about this," Margot said.

"I know, Margie, but you need to give it a rest," said Louise. "It's been five years. Mom's never going to change her mind."

Esme knew they were talking about Isabel and didn't feel up to listening to it. "Look at the sea," she said. "Isn't it calm this morning?"

Louise set a tray of coffee down on the desk. "It's pretty."

"Maybe we'll go for a swim later." Margot flopped down on the couch and smoothed her floral summer dress over her knees.

"That would be nice. Wouldn't it?" Esme smiled at Joe.

"Well, maybe. If we can catch our flight in time," said Joe.

"Flight?" Esme froze. "You booked a flight?"

"No, baby." Joe looked away. "I wouldn't do that without talking to you. I was just thinking, if the will reading is over quickly, maybe we could try to catch a redeye home tonight."

Tonight. Esme hadn't even walked through all the rooms in the mansion yet. Where would the house go now that Grammy was gone? She guessed all Grammy's assets would be liquidated and sold off to some stranger. Her heart plummeted and suddenly the whole world was spinning.

Gwen and Lance arrived a few minutes later. Gwen grunted greetings to everyone in the room, helped herself to coffee, and sat in an armchair next to Louise, who was wearing a skirt and jacket like she was going to a business meeting. Lance sat silently near Gwen, staring at the floor.

"Can you believe that Mom used some local guy to handle her estate?" Gwen scoffed scathingly. "Grammy was worth millions. She should have used a proper firm from the city."

Louise shrugged noncommittally.

Esme thought she was going to throw up when the lawyer walked in. Not that he was intimidating; in fact, he was a skinny, suntanned creature with a mop of beachy blond waves that looked like they belonged on a surfboard, not in an office. His suit was slightly rumpled, and he clutched a manila envelope with shaky hands. Gwen was cruel, Esme thought, but she was right. He did look out of his depth.

"Good morning, everyone." The lawyer cleared his throat and took his place in Grammy's high-winged leather desk chair, where he looked tiny and colorless compared to how she used to be. "I'm Reginald

Armstrong, Mrs. Hamilton's attorney. Are we all present?"

Margot opened her mouth.

"Yes, we are," said Gwen crisply.

"We are now!" someone thundered from the hallway.

"Oh no, not this guy again," Lance muttered.

Preston Langford strode into the room, swinging his silver cane. His hair was ruthlessly slicked back today, and his eyes held none of yesterday's rheuminess. Instead, they were sharp and clear, and they focused on Reginald like lasers.

"Mr. Langford," said Reginald stiffly, "this reading concerns only Mrs. Hamilton's family."

"It concerns Mrs. Hamilton's property," Preston snapped, "and that concerns me."

Esme tensed at the thought. Grammy had said that Preston was trying to buy up Mermaid Cove and build hideous developments on this beautiful land.

What if...

No, she told herself. *Surely not*.

Lance stood. "We don't need a real estate agent yet, Mr. Langford," he said calmly.

"You don't know that," Preston sneered. "I'm here to help. Dealing with Alicia's estate will be very overwhelming, and I'm here to lend you my financial expertise."

"I think it's time you left." Lance reached for Preston's arm the way he'd done at the funeral the day before.

"No," said Gwen.

Her voice rang through the room. Everyone stared at her in shock, not least Reginald.

"Gwen?" Lance said, worried.

"Let him stay," she snapped.

Margot's eyes narrowed. Esme felt the same ugly suspicion building in her chest.

"I told him about the will reading," said Gwen, confirming it.

"What! Why?" Margot said.

"He called to ask if the mansion was for sale. I said it soon would be and mentioned the will reading would be this morning. You're certainly forward, Mr. Langford, but you might as well be here. I'm her only daughter and her husband died long ago. Alicia will have left the house to me. And I can't wait to get rid of it." She glared at Preston. "If you have the money, you can buy it on the spot."

"Um," said Reginald, "that's not how—"

"An excellent idea." Preston talked over him.

"Mom, I don't think—" Louise began.

"But Mom—" Esme joined her.

"For Pete's sake, all of you, just shut up so that we can get this over with," Gwen snapped. "Preston, sit down. Reginald, go on."

Preston perched on an armchair. Margot gave him a withering scowl; Louise looked everywhere except at him. Esme was the only one who saw his cold eyes fixed on the envelope. The thought of a huge development being built where the mansion had stood made her stomach churn, and she almost got up and fled the room. Only Joe's arm around her shoulders anchored her to her chair.

"All right, then." Reginald cleared his throat again. He opened the envelope and pulled out several pages of neatly typed documents, as well as five more envelopes. These were much smaller and made of parchment paper, giving *Lord of the Rings* vibes, and Esme remembered how Grammy had taught her to make her own parchment-looking paper with coffee and a cigarette lighter. Each was sealed with a heavy wax stamp.

"What is this?" Gwen demanded.

"I'm... not sure," Reginald admitted.

"How can you not be sure? Didn't you draw up her will?"

Preston rolled his eyes.

"Gwen, darling." Lance took her hand. "Let him do his job."

Reginald was sweating. He wiped his hands on his pants and picked up the sheaf of papers.

"The last will and testament of Alicia Hamilton," he read.

Tears stung Esme's eyes. She rubbed her nose, trying to banish them, and Joe's arm tightened around her shoulders.

"I, the undersigned—" Reginald began.

The study door banged open. Esme jumped, and Gwen turned suddenly ashen, her face completely devoid of color.

"Oh, sorry," said Isabel. "Am I late?"

The black sheep of the family stood in the doorway, wearing ink black skinny jeans studded with metal spikes, combat boots, a leather jacket and a white tee shirt that hugged her scrawny figure. Her black curls exploded around her head and spilled down to her waist. Dark eye makeup and winged eyeliner, with lipstick the color of dried blood, completed the look.

Esme flew to her feet. “Izzy!” she cried. She covered the distance between them in seconds and wrapped her arms around her sister, drawing her close.

Isabel laughed, and her body softened as she returned Esme’s embrace. “It’s great to see you, Es. It really is.”

“I’m so glad you came.” Esme hugged her tighter.

“Me too.” Margot piled onto the hug. Louise got up but hovered just on the outskirts of the joyful reunion, her eyes darting to Gwen. Lance was smiling from ear to ear, but he didn’t leave his seat.

Esme stepped back. “How are you? I thought you were in San Francisco.”

“I was. We played our last show last night and I couldn’t wiggle out of it,” said Isabel. “That’s why—”

“Nonsense!” Gwen thundered.

Everyone turned to stare at her. Even Preston shrank back.

The color was rushing back to Gwen's cheeks now, cherry red. "Do you expect me to believe that you skipped your grandmother's funeral and arrived at the will reading because of a scheduling conflict?"

Isabel's eyes narrowed, but she took a deep breath, and the anger leached out of her expression. "Mom, I'm not here to fight with you. I would have been at the funeral if I could."

"Take it easy, Gwenny." Lance squeezed her hand. "Isn't it all water under the bridge by now?"

Gwen's tears spilled over. She rose to her feet, her hands clenched into fists. "Water under the bridge, Lance? *Water under the bridge*? Don't you remember what she put us through? Those days and nights of thinking that our baby girl was— was—" She couldn't finish.

Isabel's expression darkened. "I was dealing with something. I needed love and support."

"I tried, Isabel!" Gwen shrieked. "We both tried. We tried to give you everything, but you flung it back in our faces."

Reginald cleared his throat yet again. "Should I come back another time?"

"No." Gwen barked.

"Yeah, maybe." Isabel put her hands on her hips.

"Whoa, whoa. Everyone just chill." Margot made calming motions with her hands. "We can talk about this."

"I've tried talking about this, Margie." Isabel stepped back. "But right now, I don't want to talk about anything. I just want to be here in Grammy's house."

"What gives you the right to be here?" Gwen said barely containing herself. "You've made it perfectly clear you don't want anything to do with this family."

"That's garbage," Isabel shouted.

"I can see this is a bad time," Reginald said timorously.

Preston sighed and looked bored.

"Please, everyone, stop yelling," Esme begged. "Let's sit down and have some coffee."

"Your grandmother would be ashamed of you." Gwen was unrelenting.

Isabel laughed. "My grandmother welcomed me back here every holiday, Mom."

Gwen froze. "She what?"

"Yeah, she wasn't going to throw me out on my ear just because I'd made some mistakes and ended up in juvie," Isabel spat. "Not like you."

"Isabel," Lance gasped. "You know it was more complicated than that."

"You were a thief," Gwen bellowed. "We didn't know how to help you anymore."

Isabel shook her head. "I don't want to go over this with you again. I'm so done."

Esme caught Joe's eye. He sat motionless on the couch, wide-eyed, his face very still. Shame curled in Esme's gut, and her cheeks burned. She longed to apologize to him.

"Please," she said. "We don't have to do this right now. Let's relax, hear the will, and talk about this quietly."

"I want to know why she's here," Gwen said. "All these years and I've never heard a word from her. I wouldn't even have known that she's still alive if she hadn't emailed you sometimes, Esme."

"I email Esme because she treats me like a human being," Isabel yelled.

"Stop yelling," Lance thundered.

"I'll... I'll come back tomorrow," Reginald squeaked. He grabbed his papers and fled. Joe followed quietly, his shoulders hunched, his hand already raising his phone to his ear.

Preston gave the room a withering glance. "Well, I will certainly be back, too," he announced, "when this will reading can be conducted without becoming a circus." He swept out of the room.

Esme watched as Gwen and Isabel yelled at each other. She pushed past Isabel and staggered into the house, hot tears spilling over her cheeks. When had this family become a complete disaster?

And why couldn't she stop it?

Chapter Six

When Esme's blurry vision cleared, she was standing in the guests' common room on the second floor.

She stumbled over to the tall French doors that formed one side of the room. Half expecting them to be locked, she tried the handles, but they swung open when she pushed, hinges screeching. Esme staggered through them and onto the tiled balcony that overlooked the beach below. She wanted to grab the wrought-iron railing, but it was caked with bird droppings and rust, so she simply stood at the edge of the balcony instead and stared at the ocean.

Why had she come here? Automatically, she supposed. This room was where she used to sit with her parents and sisters when they came to Mermaid Cove on vacation, late in the evenings when Grammy was writing or had gone to bed and Grandpa was tired of company, which he often was. She had spent so many early Christmas mornings or late Thanksgiving evenings in this room. Before everything went wrong.

Esme exhaled, keeping her eyes trained on the ocean. The sun shimmered on its perfect surface. A fleet of seabirds floated on the water some way out. Esme wasn't sure what they were. Gulls, perhaps? Terns? She didn't know seabirds that well, even though Grandpa used to be able to name them all.

She could picture him now, pointing at a wheeling wingshadow far above the waves. *That's a double-crested cormorant, Emmy. Isn't he beautiful?*

Grammy would laugh. *Looks like a baby dragon to me!*

Maybe he is a baby dragon, in another world, Grandpa would say, and they would share a secret little smile that teenage Esme had thought was really disgusting.

Tears prickled the corners of her eyes again, and she pressed the heels of her hands against them. She was so tired of grief already, and it had been only a few days.

Wearied by the thoughts swirling around her mind, Esme turned to the common room. Now that her vision had cleared, it was plain to see that nobody had used this space in a long, long time. The comfortable, fluffy couches were caked with dust, and Esme's tracks stood out on the rug. All the curtains were closed.

The room was twilit, and one of the French doors hung slightly on one hinge. Outdated magazines littered the coffee table. Esme remembered the bookshelf at the back of the room being stacked with ornaments, toys and games, but now there were only some elderly directories and yearbooks.

It was a shame to see this space looking so neglected when her family had had so many happy times there.

She wandered over to the first of the big windows and pulled the curtains over. Dust flew into the air, and she spluttered, waving it away as she forced the windows open and allowed a gust of fresh, salty air into the room.

The burst of air instantly made her feel better, and she hurried to the other two windows. When she pulled the last curtains aside, one popped off its railing and fell to the floor.

"You needed to be washed anyway," Esme told the curtain. "You all need to be washed."

Grammy had an industrial-sized washing machine in the basement, so Esme didn't hesitate. She pulled down all the curtains one by one, then all the throws off the couches for good measure, piling them all in a heap in the corner of the room. A quick trip to the broom closet on the first floor revealed the vacuum cleaner that Grammy had always sworn by. Esme plugged it in and got to work.

She hummed as she cleaned, quickly getting rid of the dust and sand and cobwebs that had collected on the carpet, corners and ceiling. The more she worked, the more the pangs in her chest were soothed.

When she put away the vacuum, she found a can of furniture polish and a rag, then got to work on the shelves. The old books all went into a box in the attic, where she found boxes and boxes of Grammy's own books, all brand-new author copies that had never been touched. There was a huge rubber tub of random ornaments, too, treasures from Grammy's many travels: jade dragons, wooden horses, pretty shells still dusted with sand, colorful geckos made of beads.

Esme was on her hands and knees, tightening the last of the loose screws on the French door, when Joe spoke behind her. "Es? What... what are you doing?"

Esme jumped guiltily. She sat back on her heels, suddenly aware of the dust in her hair and the sweat streaking her face and arms. "Oh, Joe. Sorry, honey." She cleared her throat. "I, um, I was just... I don't know."

Joe looked around the room, his hands buried in the pockets of the cute swimming shorts she'd bought him the first summer they were dating. They were bright yellow with little purple sharks on them. The sharks wore sunglasses.

"Wow. Have you been in here all this time?"

"Yeah." Esme got up. "Are you okay? Do you need anything?"

Joe sagged onto the couch and ran a hand over the newly vacuumed throw. "Not really, no."

Esme put the screwdriver down on the polished coffee table and sat next to him. "I'm sorry about my family." She sighed. "They... they're a lot. It was chaos down there just now, and I'm really sorry you had to see that."

"It's not your fault, honey." Joe took her hand.

"I know, but I still feel bad because you've ended up in the middle of it," said Esme. "How weird was that property guy just showing up like that?"

Joe didn't seem to know what to say. He gazed around the room, his eyes dwelling on the freshly cleaned rug, the windows stripped of their curtains, offering breathtaking views over the beach, the sea, and the gardens.

The room was all wood and cream, the way Esme remembered it when she was a kid, except that she'd added pops of bright yellow here and there from her attic discoveries: cushions on the couches, a runner on the coffee table, a leaping glass dolphin on the bookshelf. Grammy's series was lined up neatly in order on the shelf.

"This room looks amazing, honey. Did you do all this?"

Esme shrugged. "I wanted to keep busy."

"Well, you did a great job." Joe smiled. "I wandered in here by accident yesterday and I thought it was a different room at first."

"Yeah," said Esme. "There are a lot of memories in this room. I think the last time I remember my family being really happy was here."

"Oh?"

"We used to come here every summer for a few weeks. Mom never really liked it, but Dad and my sisters always loved it. We used to spend half the time on the beach, of course, but when it rained, we'd all sit here and play board games. Grammy, Grandpa, my parents, all of us."

Esme smiled. "Isabel always used to win when we played Cluedo. Nobody could beat her. She always put things together so quickly. Maybe that's why Mom was so shocked when she started to struggle at school. We thought Isabel would be the book smart one."

Joe rubbed her arm. "Is that part of why she ended up falling in with the wrong crowd?"

"Who knows?" Esme sighed. "I should never have let it happen."

"It wasn't your fault, Es."

"I feel like it was. I was her big sister. I should have known something was going on."

"You were in college." Joe wrapped an arm around her. "You had no way of knowing."

"The next thing I knew, Mom was calling to tell me that Izzy was in juvenile hall for theft." Esme blinked back tears, then wiped them away and took a deep breath. "I'm sorry. I think you've had enough family drama for one day, right?"

Joe sighed. "Do you think the lawyer will be back tomorrow?"

Esme heard the prickle in his voice and her toes curled. "I'm sure he will. Then we can get the will reading out of the way. Hopefully Preston doesn't show up again."

"Good. Good." Joe nodded quickly.

Esme's gut clenched, and she begged him silently not to say anything about going straight home after the will reading. She wasn't ready to let go of this house, of Mermaid Cove, of Grammy. She tried not to imagine bulldozers leveling the grand old house and crushing the beautiful gardens under their ruthless treads.

Closing her eyes, Esme remembered how she and her sisters had laughed in this room. She'd dreamed of staying here with Joe and their own kids someday. Hearing the little ones giggle in the common room when she and Joe were still half asleep...

But they would have to leave Mermaid Cove soon. And she knew that once they left, there would never be any coming back.

Chapter Seven

ESME'S HANDS WERE CLENCHED on her knees. She sat very still on the couch beside Joe, her heart thudding painfully behind her sternum.

Isabel and Gwen sat on opposing sides of the room, avoiding looking at each other. Gwen was stiff and tight in her armchair beside Lance; Isabel took up an entire couch near the desk, sprawling, her combat boots bouncing with impatience. Esme and Joe sat with Margot and Louise in the no-man's-land near the coffee table. Margot was pale, her eyes very red; Louise scrolled through her phone, chin cupped in one hand.

Reginald almost sneaked into the room, his tail already between his legs, his manila envelope clutched under his arm.

"Good morning, everyone," he said nervously.

Gwen and Isabel glared at him.

"Good morning," said Esme.

Joe nodded. Margot wiped streaming eyes and Louise sighed and put away her phone.

"You're early," Gwen accused. "You were supposed to get here at nine-thirty."

"Yes, well." Reginald cleared his throat. "I thought it best to change the time so that we wouldn't be, ah, interrupted."

Esme thought of Preston and had to smother her grin.

"Good move, Reggie," said Isabel.

"No matter," Gwen said. "He's only an email away."

The lawyer ignored her, and Esme started to think he had more of a backbone than she'd expected.

"Shall I just get on with it, then?" Reginald asked, clutching the envelope.

"The sooner the better," said Joe.

Esme took deep breaths, feeling her palms grow slippery. This was the moment she was going to find out what would happen to the house that Grammy had loved—that Esme loved—the house that was so filled with happy memories.

A vision of this very study, the one where magic was born, being demolished flashed through her mind, the smell of wet plaster and ruined concrete replacing the rich colors and the smell of old books. She could hardly bear it.

"All right." Reginald took out the documents and began to read. "*I, the undersigned, Alicia Hamilton...*" He read out her social security number and address. "... *do hereby declare this to be my last will and testament.*"

The stuffy words sounded so unlike the Grammy that Esme knew. She sat still, listening as Reginald labored through legal jargon about revocation clauses, executors and security.

Reginald stopped suddenly.

"Well?" Gwen raised her head. "You've finally reached the part where we actually find out what to do with my mother's estate. What's the matter?"

"It's, ah." Reginald cleared his throat. "It's a little unconventional, that's all."

"What do you mean, unconventional?" Louise asked sharply.

"Guys." Isabel raised a hand. "Just let the guy read the will, okay?"

"Spoken like someone who knows this has nothing to do with her," Gwen sniped.

"Mom," Esme gasped.

Gwen glowered.

"Please, go on, Reginald," said Lance.

Reginald swallowed. "Okay. It says... well, this is what it says." He cleared his throat. "*Now that all that legal nonsense is out of the way, here's my last message to my precious family.*"

Esme sat up straight. That sounded much more like Grammy.

"*There's nothing I have left to tell you about how much I love all of you. You know that. You know that you were all my moon and stars, and I can't wait to wrap all of you in my arms again,*" Reginald read.

The mood in the room had changed instantly. Everyone smiled through their tears; even Gwen's expression had softened.

"*Now, what to do with all this stuff I'm leaving behind? You know that none of it really matters, not compared to all of you. Of everything I leave behind, only the people I love truly matter.*"

Gwen's eyes were filled with tears, her lower lip trembling.

"*For this reason, I have left everything to the five great loves of my life that I leave behind,*" Reginald read on. "*Enclosed in the envelope with this stuffy old legal document, you'll each find an envelope addressed to you. Once you open them, I promise things will be much more fun.*"

Esme stared at the five parchment envelopes lying on the desk, each with its heavy, red wax seal, and her heart skipped a beat. She thought suddenly of the elaborate scavenger hunts that Grammy would hold for her grandchildren—as well as any kids from the village who showed up—every summer. A familiar bolt of excitement rolled through her veins.

"*Before you do that, I have a message for each of you.*" Reginald cleared his throat.

Gwen lowered her head into her hands and pressed her fingers into her hair. "Oh, Mom, *why*?" she mumbled.

"*I will start with the youngest. To my dearest Margot, never forget that all the magic you need is within you and around you.*"

Margot's tears spilled over, and she brushed them away.

"*To my precious Isabel, may you never lose your propensity for charging down the road less traveled.*"

Isabel's lips twitched, her eyes filling with wistful longing.

"*To my darling Louise, always leave room for your horizons to grow wider than the seven seas.*"

Louise shook her head, smiling.

"*To my powerful Esme, may you always believe that home is where you make it.*"

Esme laughed through her tears and wrapped her arms around herself, wishing she could feel the pressure of a hug from Grammy one last time.

"*To my beautiful Gwenevere—*" Reginald began.

"I hate that name," Gwen snapped. "I hate it."

"It's all right, love." Lance rubbed her knee.

Reginald soldiered on. "*To my beautiful Gwenevere, may you fall wildly in love with everything around you once more.*"

Gwen groaned.

Reginald kept reading. "*All will become clear once you open your envelopes. I know that you will all know exactly what to do with what I'm leaving you; each piece has been carefully chosen just for you. I am so proud of you and I love you all. May you each enjoy your own hero's journey as you uncover what I have left for you.*"

"This isn't going to be straightforward, is it?" Lance said.

"*With all the love in my heart and all the joy in my soul, Grammy.*" Reginald lowered the paper, his face ashen. "That's all it says."

"Reginald." Gwen sighed. "Were you not part of setting up this will?"

"Ma'am," said Reginald, "you knew Alicia. I simply did what she told me."

"What's in the envelopes?" Esme asked.

"I don't know. Alicia never let me see," said Reginald.

Esme got to her feet, eager to hear her grandmother's words again. She hurried to the desk and her eye quickly picked out the envelope with her name in calligraphic, medieval-style font on the front.

"May I?" she asked, lifting it.

Reginald nodded. "Absolutely. It's yours."

"Have you ever heard of a will being like this?" Gwen hissed. Lance murmured to her soothingly.

Esme gently popped off the wax with her fingernail the way Grammy had taught her and opened the letter. A piece of parchment fell out, and she opened it carefully.

Grammy had written the words with her fountain pen. There were blotches and irregular spots on the paper, but Esme could easily decipher their meaning.

Where memory sleeps,

The beginning waits.

Esme turned the paper over, but there was nothing written on the back.

"Well?" said Louise. "What does it say?"

"Um." Esme turned to them. "It says, '*Where memory sleeps, the beginning waits*'."

Gwen's jaw dropped. "What?"

"That's all." Esme held the paper up to the sunlight. "I don't think there's anything else."

"Ooh." Margot clapped her hands. "It's the beginning of a riddle."

“No,” Gwen moaned. “Please, please, no. Tell me this isn’t happening.”

“What is going on?” Joe asked.

“Margot’s right.” Esme looked down at the page. “It *is* a riddle, and I think we each have one.” She laughed. “It’s just like the scavenger hunts Grammy used to make for us. We have to solve the riddles if we want to find out what our inheritance is.”

Isabel threw back her head and couldn’t contain her laughter.

“Oh, Grammy, really.” Louise shook her head.

“This is so cool,” Margot said excitedly. “I wonder what mine says.” She grabbed the envelope but didn’t open it.

“This is the most Grammy thing I’ve ever seen in my life,” Isabel laughed. “It’s amazing!”

Gwen rounded on Reginald. “This can’t be legal.” She snatched Esme’s paper and waved the parchment in his face. “This cannot be a legally binding document. Where is the real will? Is this some kind of joke?”

Reginald cowered. “Ma’am, I assure you—”

"We need to get a more experienced lawyer to look at this," Louise chipped in.

"Why?" said Isabel. "This is super cool. This is what Grammy wanted."

"We just need to solve the riddles, that's all," said Esme, taking back the parchment.

"I'm not jumping through crazy hoops for my mother ever again." Gwen's voice was shrill. "Reginald, I'm telling you, there had better be a real will back at your offices, or so help me—"

"Ma'am." Reginald made a bold effort to square his skinny shoulders. "This is the last will and testament that Alicia Hamilton left behind."

"Why would you let her do something like this?" Gwen squawked. "She was worth millions. This is just crazy."

"It's what she wanted," said Reginald, a speck of fire flashing in his eyes.

"This does seem like a lot of effort," Margot admitted. "And a little crazy. Like, shouldn't a will be all serious and everything?"

"If I knew anything about Alicia," said Reginald, "it's that she did things her own way."

"Only because her lawyer didn't know any better." Gwen threw up her hands. "Why would she hand over her estate to some small-town kid like you?"

Reginald's cheeks flushed, and he hung his head.

"This can't be right." Louise took the document from Reginald and skimmed it. "I know some excellent attorneys back in the city. I'll have them review it and let us know our options."

"Why?" Isabel demanded. "We could just solve the riddles."

"Spoken like someone with the time for silly games," Gwen sniped.

Suddenly, Esme had had enough. She rose to her feet and stepped forward.

"You know nothing about my life," Isabel snapped. "Stop pretending like you do."

"Well, that's not my fault," Gwen yelled.

"ENOUGH!"

Esme's shout surprised everyone, including herself. Joe's jaw dropped. Total silence fell on the room, and everyone stared at her, even the terrified lawyer now cowering behind the desk.

Esme's hand shook so hard that the parchment clenched between her fingers rattled, but she knew what she had to say.

"This isn't about the law," she said, quietly but firmly. "This will isn't about grabbing for stuff. None of us are desperate. We all have what we need. There's no reason for us to be greedy about this."

"Oh, Esme." Louise sighed. "If a will is not about stuff, what on earth is it about?"

"It's about what Grammy wanted." Esme pointed at the portrait on the wall behind the desk, the one she hadn't wanted to look at too closely. Her sisters had chipped in with her when they were all teenagers to commission it for Grammy and Grandpa's fiftieth wedding anniversary, and they'd both cried when they'd first seen it.

It depicted the old couple sitting on a peaceful, grassy knoll, laughing, surrounded by all the magical creatures that Grammy had so vividly imagined: fairies fluttering around, a unicorn grazing nearby, a small dragon curled up in Grammy's lap. The scene was fanciful, but the artist had captured Grammy's smile exactly, the way the laughter lines bunched up at the corners of her eyes, her crooked teeth, her pure joy.

No one spoke for a few long moments. Esme didn't try to blink back the warm, salty tears that trickled down her cheeks.

"I don't know if it's legal," she said, "and I know it's all a little crazy, but this is for certain." She held up the parchment. "This is exactly the type of thing that Grammy loved to do, and this is exactly what Grammy wanted. If we loved her at all, if we respect her memory at all, then what harm could it do to play her game and solve her riddles?"

A battery of glances bounced through the family. Gwen's fists were clenched, but Margot and Isabel both nodded. Everyone's cheeks were streaked with tears.

"Esme's right." Isabel brushed at her face with the back of her arm. "This isn't about us."

"Yeah." Louise sighed. "It's all a bit crazy, but this is exactly what Grammy wanted. I mean, that's clear."

"We should do what she wanted," Margot whimpered. "We really should."

Esme met Gwen's eyes. "Mom?"

Gwen ran a hand over her face, then stared down at the envelope in her other hand. When she sighed, she seemed to shrink six inches.

"Oh, all right," she mumbled. "I guess we'll jump through the hoops one last time."

Chapter Eight

THE SAND FELT LIKE a balm under Esme's bare feet. It pressed against aching muscles too used to being enclosed and walking on pavement, massaging the sore places between the minute bones as she strolled across the shoreline, the gentle waves lapping over her toes from time to time. She'd let her hair down and the breeze finger-combed it, tickling her scalp.

She'd wandered across the deep lawn in front of the house without a plan after lunch, but now wished she'd brought her bathing suit. If she had, she could have waded into these waves, then dived beneath the salt water and thrown all of her sorrow and tension into the ocean.

The warm hands on her shoulders startled her, but she only tensed for a moment before she recognized the landscape of those soft fingers, the smell of the crisp cologne that reached her nostrils.

"Hey, babe." Esme opened her eyes.

Joe squeezed her shoulders, pressing his thumbs into the two knots on either side of her neck that always appeared when she was stressed. "You okay?"

"Yeah." Esme sighed. "Just... wanted to get rid of some tension."

Joe rubbed the knots, bringing pleasant release. "This morning was rough, but I'm so proud of you. You said the right thing."

Esme tipped her head back, and he kissed the top of it. "You think that it's all a bit crazy, too."

Joe laughed. "Maybe, but you weren't wrong. Alicia would have wanted this."

Esme turned to him and extended a hand. He took it easily, brushing his thumb across the back of her hand, and they strolled over to the wooden bench that Grammy had bought and installed at the edge of the tide line when Grandpa could no longer walk so far. The smooth timber was warm on Esme's bare knees when she sat.

"I don't understand why Mom is so resistant to everything that Grammy did," said Esme.

Joe sat beside her and wrapped an arm around her shoulders. "I guess she has to have her reasons."

"She always talks about how she hated growing up as the weird writer's kid. There were rough times when she was a kid, too. Times when Grandpa tried to get Grammy to get a job, but she never stopped believing in her books."

"Well." Joe gestured at the mansion behind him. "That paid off, right?"

"Yeah, but Mom was an older teenager by then." Esme shrugged. "I guess she never really benefited from it, in her mind."

"That makes sense, I suppose," said Joe. "It was nice to see Isabel."

Joe and Isabel had met briefly at the wedding reception. Isabel snuck away before anyone else could notice she was there.

"Yeah, it's so great to spend time with her again," said Esme. "Actually, I know we've been arguing, but it's nice to have everyone together again. That hasn't happened in years."

Joe nodded.

"In fact, I think that's why Grammy set up her will the way she did."

"And here I was thinking that maybe the sweet old girl was going a little crazy toward the end."

Esme couldn't tell if he was joking or not, so she pushed away the sting of offense she felt at the words. "I think Grammy was trying to *make* us all spend time in Mermaid Cove. She wanted to bring us together. It was her last effort at making her family whole again."

"Mm," Joe grunted. "Maybe."

Silence fell. Esme could only wish that she could tell what he was thinking.

"I have a conference call." Joe squeezed her hand. "I'll make dinner."

"Thanks, babe," Esme said. "I think I'll walk a little longer."

Joe left, and Esme stood on the beach, gazing at the calm waves lapping onto the shore. A dolphin's fin broke the surface, and she whirled around to call out to Joe and show him, but he was already head down, staring at his phone as he returned to the mansion. She gave up. Instead, she watched the pod of dolphins splashing past alone as the mansion door clanged shut, the sound echoing across the long lawn.

The hum of a large engine broke her daydream as the dolphins played and bounded into the distance. She turned as the big silver Rolls purred to a halt on the grass a few hundred feet away.

Esme sighed. She didn't have the energy for Preston Langford now, and she started toward the house, wanting to call Lance and get him to chase the old man off. But when he unfolded from the Rolls' backseat, there were tears on his cheeks.

Esme stopped. "Mr. Langford?" she called. "Are you okay?"

"Oh, hello there." Preston pulled a silk handkerchief from the pocket of his elegant gray suit. "I'm sorry. I didn't see you here on the beach... I thought I'd be alone."

Esme frowned. "I'm afraid this is private property."

"I know, I know. I'm sorry." Preston sighed. "I just... She feels nearer when I'm here, you know?"

Esme tilted her head as the old man strode toward her, his stick digging into the sand.

"How well did you know my grandma?" she asked.

"How well?" Preston smiled. His gaze darted over her briefly, then landed on the horizon. "I loved her," he said softly.

Esme blinked. "She... she never said that."

"She didn't?" Preston's eyes narrowed.

Esme shook her head. "She only mentioned that, uh, that you're a real estate developer in the area."

"Ah." Preston leaned on his stick. "Yes. Ali and I certainly had differing opinions on that. But we were more than that, you know."

Esme was startled. Her grandpa had died five years ago. She supposed it wouldn't be that odd for Grammy to start seeing someone again, but it felt incomprehensible. Grandpa had been Grammy's universe, her sun and moon and stars. No one could ever be that again.

"You and Grammy were... seeing each other?" she asked.

"Yes, a long, long time ago." Preston laughed softly. "When we were in high school."

"Oh," said Esme, relieved. Grammy had married Grandpa when she was twenty-five.

"Yes. We went to the same school. The best private school in San Diego. My parents sent me there, but Alicia got there on her own merit. She had a rare scholarship to the school. I thought she was pure magic."

Esme smiled. "She was pure magic."

"Splendid, wasn't she? Absolutely splendid." Preston sighed. "Things didn't work out between us in the end, but for me, she was always the one who got away. I don't think I ever fell out of love with your grandmother... it's Esme, right?"

"Yes."

"I don't think I ever fell out of love with Alicia," Preston repeated quietly. "I'll never stop missing her. Never."

Esme hugged herself. She wondered if this old man had been lonely for the sixty years since high school. He wore no wedding ring. Much as she'd adored Grandpa, she felt a brief pang of empathy for Preston, pining after Grammy all his life.

"I don't blame you," she said. "Everyone who met Grammy loved her. She was that kind of person... magic to everyone."

"I know exactly what you mean." Preston sighed. "I hope you don't think I'm rude for coming to the will reading. I want to do whatever I can to help your family, Esme. It's the last thing I have left to do for sweet Alicia. I would love to own the land she loved one day."

Esme stared at him. She wanted to ask if he was going to bulldoze her beautiful mansion and build a complex on it, but she swallowed the rude question quickly.

"I hear the will was read again," said Preston.

From who? Esme wondered but didn't ask. "Yes, it was."

"And?" Preston asked. "Who did she leave the property to? Should I speak to your mother about it?"

Esme shook her head. "We don't know yet. It's... complicated." She laughed. "Grammy left us each a riddle to solve before we can find out what she left each of us."

"A riddle?" Preston clenched his jaw, a muscle jumping in his cheek.

"Yes. Isn't that just like Grammy?" Esme laughed again. "We'll find out soon enough, I'm sure."

"Yes. Yes, it is just like her."

He fell silent and stared at the ocean for a few moments longer. Then he whirled around, stalked to his car, and was gone.

Chapter Nine

ESME STOOD ON TIPTOE on the stepladder, reaching for the topmost shelf. Cobwebs tickled her fingers, making goosebumps rise on her neck and shoulders, but she pushed through and gripped the edge of a book at the back of the shelf.

"Gotcha!" She pulled the book down and stepped off the ladder, panting with effort.

At this time in the afternoon, Grammy's library was always bathed in sunlight as the sun streamed through the enormous bay windows on the seaward side of the room.

Considering how many books Grammy had in her study, it seemed impossible that she needed a whole other room for them, but the shelves were crammed so tight, Esme had to use all her strength to pull some off.

She blew dust off the cover of this one and sat down on the rug in front of the shelf, where she'd arranged the other books in neat stacks by category and then, alphabetically, by order. Grammy had just shoved them in willy-nilly but had probably known exactly where to find every single one.

She would definitely have been able to find this one, Esme thought, wiping down the cover with a damp cloth. It was an ancient copy of *Ferdinand*, with a little gold-leaf bull frolicking on the red leather cover, and Grammy had read it to Esme over and over until its spine cracked.

When Esme opened the book, she could find the spot where Grandpa had fixed her favorite page with tape. She smiled and ran her fingers down the old, yellowed scrap of tape. "But not Ferdinand," she said.

The library door creaked, and Esme looked up. Joe wandered in, looking lost and awkward in his still-dry swimming trunks. Esme didn't think he'd ever actually used them. His hands were deep in the pockets, and he paused in the doorway to look around the library.

"Doing some more organizing, huh?" he asked.

The weirdness that had hung in the air between them on the beach this morning clearly hadn't changed. Esme could feel it settling queasily in her belly.

"Yeah, I thought I'd rearrange Grammy's books. In case someone else wanted to read them." She held up the book. "This was my favorite when I was a kid. Grammy read it to me all the time."

Joe shuffled nearer and looked down at the cover. "Cute."

The word made Esme bridle, but she tried to hide it. She finished wiping down the cover and went to place it on the stack of children's books, then hesitated and put it to one side instead. Maybe *Ferdinand* could come home with her and remind her of Grammy.

She pushed the thought of going home away. This place felt more like home than anywhere else ever had; she wished she could sit here and soak up this sunshine for another twenty years.

"Look at this." Esme fished in a stack of encyclopaedias instead. "How old do you think this is?" She handed Joe a heavy leather-bound book.

He took it but made no effort to open it or guess. "So, uh, Es, I was thinking..."

Esme swallowed her nerves. "Yes?"

Joe cleared his throat. "I'd like to book our flights back."

Esme's gut clenched.

"Do you want to leave in the morning, or should I book for the afternoon instead?"

"Wait. You... you want to book our flights for tomorrow?"

"Well, when else? That way I can still fit in a couple of days of work before the weekend."

"You've been working since we got here, Joe. You've barely been able to look up from your laptop."

Joe's expression hardened. "What do you want me to do? With you waiting on that client, it's not like we have any other income."

We don't need that much *income, Joe!* Esme wanted to scream. Instead, she sucked in a deep breath. "Thing is, Joe, I haven't gotten started on Grammy's riddle yet. I was thinking about it now, and—"

"Wait." Joe held up a hand. "You want to do this riddle thing now?"

His choice of words cut through Esme's heart. "When else did you think I was going to?"

"I don't know, Es," said Joe, frustrated. "Maybe at a time when normal people spend days and days at the beach, like over Thanksgiving."

Last Thanksgiving, Joe had been at the office every single day except for the holiday itself. Esme had to bite her tongue to keep herself from reminding him of that.

He saw the look on her face, though, and let his hands fall back by his sides. "I'm sorry, honey. I just didn't realize that you wanted to do this all before we go back home, but I think you need to look at this reasonably. It's not realistic."

"Not realistic?" Esme echoed.

"I've been keeping up with work online, but my boss is starting to make noises about my absence in the office." Joe took her hand. "You know I need to get back. I have to make a good impression, or there's no chance I'll get anywhere."

Where do you want to get, Joe? Esme wondered desperately. *Where is it you want to go that's so much more important than right here, right now, with me?*

"You understand, don't you?" said Joe. "So, do you want to fly out in the morning, or in the evening? I was thinking we could stay for breakfast so that you can say goodbye to everyone, then we'll still be home in time to grab something for dinner before—"

"I'm not ready to go back." Esme hadn't planned the words; they just fell out of her.

Joe blinked. "What?"

"I'm not ready to go back, Joe." Esme ripped her hand out of his grasp. "I'm just not ready."

She turned and rushed out of the library before he could stop her.

Earlier, Esme had dragged some of the wrought-iron garden furniture up the steps and onto the balcony of the common room. She'd unearthed a bunch of old cushions in the attic and added them to the furniture, thinking how cheerful they looked.

Now, they were soaked with her tears. She curled up in a chair, a cushion clasped to her face, her sobs ebbing slowly.

The thought of going back to that Chicago apartment, with its absolute silence, felt like a knife in her belly. Only this time, she wouldn't be able to pick up the phone and call Grammy when she was lonely.

She'd have no one.

Esme wiped away her tears and took deep breaths, trying to calm herself down. Joe was right, wasn't he? He needed to focus on his career. Didn't he? She'd known he was driven, that this was important to him, before she married him. This was something she had to live with.

Right?

She reached into her pocket for her phone, and her hand brushed something that crinkled like paper. When Esme fished it out, it was the piece of parchment on which Grammy had written her riddle.

Where memory sleeps,

the beginning waits.

The sight of Grammy's calligraphy made the lump in her throat grow again. Esme swallowed it down and sighed. If she only had this evening to try to solve her riddle, she might as well use it.

"Where memory sleeps," she murmured. Did Grammy mean a photograph? There were pictures all over this house, but somehow memory didn't sleep in those pictures. It was colorful. It danced.

A sleeping memory? That sounded like something that would be in a dusty box. A keepsake, maybe, like Grammy's old wedding dress, which the four sisters had found once in its garment bag in the attic. Grammy had come up there to find them taking turns to try it on. She hadn't been mad. She'd put it on herself and twirled in front of a dusty old mirror while the girls laughed and laughed.

Poor old Preston. His unrequited love tugged at Esme's heart, but nobody in the world except Grandpa Rod could ever have made Grammy that happy. She remembered how she'd twirled like a young girl in that attic, vibrant as she'd been as a bride.

The attic. Esme sat up. It was worth a try, she guessed.

Ten minutes later, Esme was in the quiet, dusty space beneath the mansion's rafters. She'd always thought that the attic was a little magical, and nothing had changed, even though she'd disturbed much of the dust and cobwebs over the past two days while she was digging out bits of furniture and decor for the common room.

Rows of square windows let in the evening sun, set in little gables in the profoundly slanting roof. It was tall in the middle, but Esme couldn't straighten up on the edges of the room.

She pushed her way between the precarious stacks of boxes, Grammy and Grandpa's handwriting clumsily labeling each. Esme noticed that there were six boxes marked *Gwenevere's Drawings.* She opened one and peered inside; the page on the top, faded with age, was a clumsy crayon rendition of a little family standing outside a castle. The little girl, whose curls matched Gwen's, wore a bright yellow crown.

"What happened to you, Mom?" Esme murmured. She replaced the box's lid carefully and rested a hand on top of it. What was going to happen to all of these drawings when the inheritance was sorted out and the house was finally sold? Maybe they'd be bulldozed alongside the mansion. The thought saddened Esme.

Her phone hummed in her pocket. Esme snatched it up, half desperate, thinking Joe might be trying to call her, but her phone's screen displayed an unknown number.

A new client, maybe? Esme wasn't in the mood to think about work, but she raised it to her ear anyway. "Esme Gordon speaking, how can I help you?"

"Hi, Esme?" The voice was familiar. "It's Reginald Armstrong. Your grandmother's lawyer."

"Oh." Esme straightened. "Hi, Reginald. Is there a problem with Grammy's will?"

"No, no. Well… not exactly. I'm sorry to disturb you. Corrie from the bookstore gave me your number. She thought I should speak to you."

"Sure. I know Corrie well. What can I do for you?"

"Well, I'm embarrassed to ask, but I noticed that the atmosphere was, uh, somewhat heated during the will reading," Reginald said.

Esme groaned. "It's okay, Reginald. You don't have to be delicate about it. It was a complete disaster, and I freely admit it."

Reginald gave an uneasy chuckle. "I understand that I don't always inspire great confidence. Maybe I'm still inexperienced, but Alicia believed in me. She paid my way through law school, you know. I'd do anything for her."

Esme smiled. "That sounds like Grammy."

"Yes, well." Reginald cleared his throat. "The reason I called is to ask, well… I've been informed that someone's lodged an official complaint against me."

"What? What does that mean for you? Are you suspended?"

"Not currently." Reginald sighed. "It's not a good thing for my career, either way, but I… was wondering if you think perhaps your mother…" He trailed off.

Esme bit her lip. "You're thinking someone in my family lodged the complaint."

"It's not impossible. I'm sorry to ask, but—"

"I understand," said Esme, "and I don't blame you for asking, but I don't actually think it was anyone in my family. Margot, Louise, and Isabel are all more than happy to do Grammy's will. We all agree that this is what she wanted."

"And, ah, Mrs. Hamilton?" Reginald asked.

Esme sighed. "Mom? I don't think she'd make a complaint, either. She turned out to be happy to go with Grammy's will, too. I don't see why she'd do it."

"All right." Reginald exhaled. "Thank you, Esme. You've been kinder than I expected."

"You know, I can think of someone else who might have done it," Esme chipped in.

"Oh?" said Reginald. "Who?"

Esme bit her lip. "Preston. Preston Langford."

A long pause stretched between them.

"I hope not," said Reginald quietly, "because if he pursues the complaint, then my career is toast. Preston gets whatever he wants."

A sudden chill ran down Esme's spine. "What do you mean?"

"Just that he has a way of bending reality to his will." Reginald said. "But I wouldn't be a lawyer at all if it wasn't for Alicia, Esme. Don't worry. I'll defend her will with everything I have."

"Thanks, Reginald. I'm sorry to hear about your trouble."

"It's okay. I'll figure it out. Thanks for hearing me out," said Reginald, and hung up.

Esme sat still for a long few minutes, staring at the boxes. What if Preston really had lodged the complaint about poor Reginald? Would he stoop so low? Maybe she was misjudging a grieving old man.

She shook the thoughts away, turned her back on the boxes, and scanned the room, trying to decide where Grammy would have hidden the next clue. *Where memory sleeps, the beginning waits.* A suit of armor stood on the far side of the room; next to it was a giant antique hat stand, hung with all sorts of decorative bird cages. Esme had no idea why Grammy had them. Keeping anything in a cage wasn't Grammy's style.

Next to the hat stand was a pile of old hardbacks with ugly, cheap dust covers, the artwork questionable. Grammy had always complained that the character on the cover didn't look anything like Tardin of Merrabor. They were the first run of her first book, the one that never really succeeded.

"The beginning waits," Esme realized out loud.

Excitement pulsed through her. She scrambled across the attic, stepping over boxes of old manuscripts and random Halloween decorations. Right behind the stack of books, her eye caught on her own name. It was written on a parchment label attached with a piece of string to a little wooden chest.

Esme pushed the books aside and crouched down in front of the chest. It looked like something that had fallen out of book six—the one where Tardin of Merrabor had to rescue the fairy king from an island of bloodthirsty pirates—in miniature.

The chest was no bigger than the carry-on suitcase Esme had brought onto the plane, but it was beautifully made, all polished mahogany held together by iron plates. The top curved like a real pirate's chest, and it had a massive iron clasp on the front, held shut by a heavy bronze padlock. Esme tugged at the padlock, but it was firm and immovable.

She picked up the label instead. Her name was the only thing written on the front, but when she flipped it over, Grammy's calligraphic writing dotted the back.

Well done, fairy.

Play to open.

Open to play.

Esme laughed out loud. "Oh, Grammy."

She couldn't wait to figure out what the second part of the riddle meant, and she knew exactly who would be able to help her think outside the box: Joe. Maybe this would convince him that they needed to stay.

Chapter Ten

ESME CLATTERED DOWN THE long hallway to the kitchen at the back of the mansion. "Joe," she called. "Joe, honey, you won't believe what I've found."

She burst into the kitchen, which always felt like it had been frozen in the eighteenth century. Grandpa had been the one who enjoyed cooking—Grammy had been capable but reluctant—and he didn't believe in what he called the "new-fangled gadgets these days". Grandpa didn't even own a mixer; he did everything by hand, including making toast and washing dishes. There were no sleek appliances in this kitchen, only a massive old wooden table, elegant cabinets lining the walls, an enormous double sink, and an old red refrigerator that stuck out like a sore thumb. The stove was gas-powered, with a huge oven in which Grandpa had cooked many excellent Sunday roasts.

Gwen looked up as Esme rushed in. She noticed her mother's face was pale, her eyes rimmed with red. The lines around her forehead and mouth seemed to have deepened in the space of two days. She hastily shoved something in the pocket of her practical but boring jeans; Esme guessed it was the piece of parchment on which Grammy had written Gwen's riddle.

"Oh, sorry, Mom." Esme stopped. "I thought Joe was in here. He said he'd make dinner."

"Yes, I was going to help him with that, but we're out of garlic and canned tomatoes." Gwen cleared her throat. "He went into Mermaid Cove with your father for a few things."

"Okay." Esme swallowed. "Cool."

Gwen tilted her head to one side. "Is everything okay with you and Joe, honey?"

"What? Yes." Esme put the chest down on the end of the table; it was lighter than she'd expected, but still heavy. "Everything's fine."

Gwen leaned back in her chair and studied her for a few moments. "I'm sorry I've been... weird ever since we got here. I've hardly even had a conversation with you."

Esme shrugged. "I know this hasn't been easy for you, Mom."

"Nothing with your grandmother was ever easy, honey." Gwen sighed, then shook her head. "But never mind that now. Sit down. I'll make some coffee."

Esme sat, a little warily, her arms folded across her chest. Gwen put the kettle on the stove and lit the hob.

"When are you guys going home?" she asked.

"I'm not sure. Joe wants to get back tomorrow."

"I'm guessing you want to stay longer," said Gwen.

Esme nodded.

"You never could get enough of this place." Gwen laughed softly. "When we came here on vacation, you used to cry your eyes out every time we left. It was like you felt more at home here than at our actual home."

Esme smiled. "It's still true."

"Yeah, well." Gwen sighed. "Margot doesn't know when she'll leave yet. Louise already booked her flight back; she's got a meeting with a client tomorrow."

Neither of them mentioned Isabel.

"What about you?" Esme asked. "When are you guys leaving?"

"I don't know." Gwen poured the coffee and placed a mug next to Esme. It was black with sugar, the way she hadn't liked it since she was an emo teenager. "I just want to go home, but your dad thinks we should spend the week here. I don't see the point."

"You've been working hard, Mom. The break could do you good."

"Well, maybe. I'm just tired, Es. I want to go home. I want to forget about... all this."

Esme tapped her fingers on the chest, not knowing what to say. She wished she could understand why her mother was so angry with Grammy. It was like Grammy dying had only made her angrier.

"Anyway." Gwen slurped her coffee. "What do you have there?"

"The next step in my riddle, I think." Esme took off the label and handed it to Gwen. "I found it in the attic."

"*Where memory sleeps.*" Gwen shook her head. "Only Mom would have come up with that." She frowned. "What's this supposed to mean?"

"I guess I have to open it, but I can't figure out how. Do you think she's hidden a key somewhere?"

"I suppose she must have, although the wording doesn't make sense. *Play to open.* She said *open*, not *unlock*."

"Oh, good thinking, I didn't even notice that."

"Maybe there's some other way to open it without undoing the padlock." Gwen fiddled with the clasp. "But what do you have to play?"

"Music?" Esme guessed. "Is there such a thing as a sound-activated lock?"

"Don't be absurd." Gwen scoffed. She turned the chest over and ran her hands over the wood. "Maybe there's some sort of game or puzzle you have to solve hidden on the outside."

"On the bottom?" Esme suggested.

They gripped the chest together and flipped it over, but the bottom was a featureless wood base, encrusted with dust and cobwebs.

"Mmm. No such luck, I guess." Gwen turned the chest back over. "What if you shake it?"

Esme picked it up and gave it a shake. Something rattled on the inside, a wooden sound, like dice.

"That's weird," said Gwen.

"I know." Esme laughed. "It's fun, though."

Gwen's lip quirked, but she didn't agree out loud.

Esme sat cross-legged on the spacious four-poster bed. Joe didn't like the canopy—she knew he thought it was ridiculous—so the curtains were drawn back and tied to the posts with the ornate silver ropes that matched the designs on the brocade bed cover. Soft white sheets crinkled as Esme shifted her position to turn the chest onto its side. Her damp hair tickled her neck, freshly washed, and the window was closed against mosquitoes.

She ran her hands over the side of the chest, poking and prodding, but only the grain of wood and the cold steel met her touch.

"There's got to be treasure inside you," she said.

Joe walked into the room from the en-suite, vigorously toweling his hair. "What did you say?"

"Oh, sorry." Esme smiled. "I was talking to the chest."

Joe raised his eyebrows but said nothing. He buttoned up his silky pajama top, hung up the towel and slipped into bed next to Esme. For a moment, he looked at the chest, and she thought he'd ask. Gwen had told him only the basics over dinner. Instead, he sighed and picked up his phone.

Esme turned the chest onto its other side, padlock down, and felt over the wood. The silence hung over them both like Joe's wet towel.

"So." Esme cleared her throat. "Have you booked our flights yet?"

Joe didn't look up from his phone. "Nope."

Esme's belly knotted at his tone, overwhelming the brief pang of relief. She kept her eyes on the chest. Was that a knot of wood, or a hidden button? She pressed it. It was just a knot of wood.

"Esme." Joe breathed. "Listen, I'm sorry about this afternoon."

Esme looked up. Joe's eyes were gentle, and he put his phone down, then reached over to wrap his hands around hers.

"I know what Alicia meant to you," he said, "and I didn't treat you with much understanding earlier.

This has to be really hard for you. I'm sorry, baby. I shouldn't have been so harsh."

Esme exhaled, a knot of tension unraveling in her chest. "Thanks, Joe. I know it's a little weird for you, since you never really knew your grandparents."

"It's not something I've experienced, but I can understand that you're grieving. I can tell this riddle means a lot to you, not because of the inheritance, but because of Grammy."

Esme nodded, unable to stop tears welling. "It feels like one last game to play with her, Joe. I know that once we leave... well... it feels like we'll never be back."

"What do you mean?"

"I guess Mom will get the house." Esme cleared her throat. "And she'll sell it and I'll never see it again."

"Oh, Essie." Joe squeezed her hand. "That doesn't have to be the case. We could come to Mermaid Cove for a weekend and stop by the house or something. It might not be that simple."

"Maybe not." Esme tried to smile. "But if Preston flattens it to the ground..."

Joe grimaced. "I'm sorry."

Esme shook her head. "I'm being ridiculous."

"No, not at all. You're going through something really hard, and it's okay to feel this way." Joe kissed her cheek. "I'm here for you. I want you to know that."

"Thanks, babe." Esme sighed.

Joe squeezed her hand lightly. "But we can't stay here forever, honey," he said, gently. "You know that."

Tears stung Esme's eyes. "I know."

"We need to get back to real life," Joe added.

Real life? Esme wasn't sure how their apartment in the city and Joe's work and her occasional coffee dates at chic cafés with her clients were any more real than the sound of the waves outside, the family dinner they'd just shared, or the feeling of sand between her toes.

She clutched the chest tightly, and something moved under her hand.

"Oh," she yelped.

"What?" Joe leaned closer.

Esme squinted. In the glow of her bedside lamp, she saw it: the faint indentation on the chest, sharply outlined.

"I don't know." She pressed it again, and a tiny drawer slid back into the chest.

"Whoa, what's in there?"

Esme pressed harder, and the drawer clicked back. When she withdrew her hand, it slid smoothly out from the chest with a soft wooden sound. It was small—a teaspoon wouldn't have fit inside—and contained only a tiny roll of parchment tied with a purple ribbon.

"The next clue?" Joe guessed.

"Yes." Esme laughed. She pulled out the roll and untied the ribbon.

"Well done, babe." Joe rubbed her back. "I can't believe you found it. It was so well hidden."

Esme unrolled the note and read.

Played to open,

not yet unlocked for playing.

The village will hook you up with the key.

"The key," said Joe. "You're nearly done."

"I guess so." Esme grinned. "The key must be somewhere in Mermaid Cove."

"Would it still be there, though?" Joe frowned. "I mean, where would you hide a key?"

"Oh, Grammy knew everyone in that village. She was friends with the whole world, it felt like. I'm sure she left the key with somebody there. All I have to do is go to the village and ask around."

Joe bit his lip and glanced at his phone.

"It's okay, babe. If we really have to go back tomorrow..."

"No... no." Joe shook his head. "I can do one more day online, I guess."

"Really?" Esme brightened.

"I can see what this means to you, honey." Joe smiled.

"Why don't you come to the village with me? You'd enjoy it."

Joe frowned. "I have an online meeting at ten."

"Most things are open by eight at this time of year, with all the tourists. We could be back in time for your meeting," Esme cajoled. "Come on, Joe? I'd love to have you with me. It would be some quality time together."

Joe's shoulders sagged. "Okay, let's do it."

"Great." Esme grinned.

Joe didn't return her smile. He kissed her cheek and rolled onto his other side, then switched off his bedside lamp so that only the bluish glow of his phone came from his side of the room.

Chapter Eleven

Mermaid Cove's sidewalk was sandy. It crunched under Esme's sandals as she ambled into the town, only ten minutes' walk from the mansion, her hand clutched loosely in Joe's. A crisp breeze lifted Esme's hair, but despite the early hour, her hand was already turning sweaty in Joe's fingers.

"Is it always this quiet?" Joe asked.

"It gets busier when all the tourists get out of bed."

Mermaid Cove was little more than a single paved street, a branch of a minor road heading down the coast, with a few small homes clustered around its edges and trails leading down to beachside properties, resorts, and RV parks.

All the businesses in town lined the main street, which didn't have a name; it was just "the main street". Every shop was painted a different color, so that the street was a cheerful mishmash of pastels that Grammy had always loved. Even the firehouse was cherry red, with the single firetruck dozing in the driveway.

No vehicles stirred on the street except for a delivery van parked outside the grocery store, a hefty farmer unloading wheels of fresh cheese from inside.

Most of the wares in the shop windows had a maritime theme: fishing tackle and boat parts, swimwear and beach towels, a rack of surfboards outside a shop painted bright blue, the boards brightly waxed, splashed with bold designs.

A bike bell rang, and three kids on bicycles zoomed past, laughing as they shoved each other playfully, beach towels streaming from their handlebars. The street forked near the end; one paved path continued down the coast, but the other turned to sand and ended at the beach, close enough that barefoot tourists could wander up for an ice cream at the grocery store before returning to the waves.

"Want an iced coffee?" Esme suggested. "The café will be open."

"The same café where we ate the other day?"

Esme laughed. "The only café. Well, unless you count Coral Kitchen just outside town, the fancy place."

"Two places to eat in the whole town." Joe laughed. "I guess they have to do everything if they're the only one, right?"

"So, iced coffee?"

"Maybe later. You know, I bet your grandma left the key with the bookstore lady who was at the funeral. With the funny name."

"Oh, Corrie." Esme laughed. "She's South African, and you're probably right. Corrie was in on most of Grammy's schemes."

They continued down the street, small shells breaking under their shoes, to the bookstore halfway down. It was painted shocking purple and had beautiful gleaming wooden French doors. *Mermaid Reads,* the sign over the door declared. A slightly newer sign had been added below it: *The Home of Alicia Hamilton!*

"I guess having a bestselling author live here put the place on the map, huh?" Joe said.

“I think Corrie was just really proud of Grammy,” said Esme. “They were friends for years before Grammy moved out here and helped Corrie to buy the store. Corrie used to be a librarian and Grammy used to sit in the library, working. They ended up as friends.”

“That’s sweet,” said Joe.

The doors were already open, and Esme stepped into the tiny, poky bookstore, the shelves crowded claustrophobically together. Cardboard cutouts from the cover of Grammy’s latest book stood at the end of one shelf. A display of travel guides was in the window; there were several posters on the wall, most of them featuring *Tales of Otherworld* titles. A huge map of Otherworld sprawled across the back wall, right above the counter where Corrie sat curled up in an armchair, sipping coffee and reading a book, her cat curled up in her lap.

The cat was round and ginger, and he hopped down from Corrie’s lap with a friendly meow as Esme and Joe came in. Corrie lowered the book.

“Hello, Esme,” she said brightly. “How are you two today?”

"We're good, thanks." Esme leaned on the counter. "How about you?"

"Oh, you know." Corrie's smile slipped. "Trying to find out how the world works without her in it, you know?" She held up the book; it was Grammy's obscure first novel. "Her words comfort me."

Joe smiled sympathetically.

"I'm sure they do," said Esme. "They comfort me, too." She'd been listening to one of the audiobooks while she cleaned the library.

"That's how it is, isn't it?" Corrie sighed and put the book to one side.

"I'll give you two a minute." Joe smiled. "Is it too early for ice cream? I saw a place selling them across the street."

"That'd be amazing. Thanks, babe," said Esme.

She asked for a popsicle and Corrie requested something with lots of chocolate, and Joe left.

"He's a gem, that one." Corrie watched him go.

Esme's gut knotted. "It's been hard to be sure of that sometimes, lately," she admitted, then stopped, shocked she'd blurted it out. It was the kind of thing she would normally only have said to Grammy.

Corrie smiled sympathetically. "I've been a crazy old cat lady all my life, dear." She stroked the cat and ginger fur wafted into the air. "But I saw your grandmother and Rod go through a few tough times of their own."

"You did? I don't remember them being anything but wildly happy."

"Wild happiness is usually built on a strong foundation of disagreement, shared suffering, arguments, and courageous love," said Corrie. "Rod and Alicia were no different."

Esme paused, her smile growing. "I guess I'll still always believe that they were a love story for the ages."

"So will you and Joe be, dear. He's the Rod to your Alicia."

Esme leaned on the counter, suddenly curious. "Corrie, did Grammy ever mention Preston to you?"

"Oh," Corrie scoffed. "That dreadful old man. He would have turned my dear bookstore into an apartment building."

Esme laughed. "Grammy mentioned that once. You know him, then?"

"Everybody in Mermaid Cove knows Preston," Corrie growled. "He's tried to buy all of us out. He wants to turn Mermaid Cove into a dreadful bunch of cheap complexes and hotels. All because of what happened between him and Alicia more than fifty years ago, of course. Utterly absurd."

Esme tilted her head. "What happened? He told me that he and Grammy were together in high school and it didn't work out."

"Oh, it was far more than that, dear," said Corrie darkly. "They dated briefly. He was very handsome and romantic, you know, and Alicia got caught up in it all. She told me it was several months before the scales fell from her eyes and she realized how foolish it was to be with him. He was condescending, arrogant, and obsessed with her."

Esme swallowed. "Obsessed?"

"Not in a good way, dear. She left him, and it went all wrong after that. I know in the end she had a restraining order against him," said Corrie. "He left her well alone while Rod was alive, apart from hounding Mermaid Cove for property. It got worse when we lost dear Rod. But she never let him bother her."

Esme shook her head, trying to imagine the sweet old man on the beach doing anything that required a restraining order. "It seems so hard to believe."

"That old fool is bad news," said Corrie firmly. "You'd do well to stay away from him."

The bell over the door jingled, and Joe walked in with the ice creams.

"You're a star, dear," said Corrie, taking hers.

Esme's fingers brushed his as she took her ice cream, sending a familiar thrill through her. She smiled at him, hoping Corrie was right.

"How can I help you, my dears?" Corrie prompted.

"Well, do you know anything about Grammy's will?" Esme asked.

Corrie cackled. "I'd almost forgotten. She told me she was going to lead the lot of you on a merry chase." Her eyes sparkled. "How did your mother take it?"

"Not well," said Esme.

"It'll do her good, you know that." Corrie leaned on the counter. "I'm not giving out any hints, though."

"So you know the answers?" Joe asked.

"No hints," said Corrie firmly.

"Okay." Esme stifled a laugh. "We were wondering if you had something for us, though. Grammy's last riddle said we could find a key in the village."

"I'm afraid not, my dear. No keys here."

"Do you know who might have one?" asked Joe.

"No hints." Corrie winked. "But maybe a little advice. If you're stuck, go through the riddle again. The answer lies in the question."

Giggles announced the arrival of three little boys, clamoring for the latest comic book, and Joe and Esme stepped aside so that Corrie could hand out the plastic-wrapped titles.

They stepped onto the sidewalk, and Joe's hands were in his pockets again. He checked his watch. "What do you think we should do next, babe?"

Esme's eye caught on the beach, where the kids from earlier had left their bikes and were splashing at the edge of the waves.

"Look at them." She pointed, laughing.

Joe followed her finger. "Looks like they're having a great time."

"They're so cute. Don't you think?"

Joe was silent, then cleared his throat and turned away. “Where do you think we should try now?”

“The answer lies in the question,” Esme murmured. She fished the page out of the pocket of her favorite summer dress—favorite precisely because it had pockets—and reread the riddle.

The village will hook you up with the key.

“Hook you up,” Esme whispered. She raised her eyes and looked straight toward the shop opposite. Its walls were bright green, and a huge metal fishhook jutted above the doorway. *Bernie’s Tackle,* the sign announced.

“Hook.” Esme turned to Joe. “I know where the key is. Come on.”

She grabbed his hand and hurried across the street to the tackle store. Its revolving doors spun wildly as she crashed inside. This place was easily twice the size of the bookstore; it was large and cool, with solemn gray walls, and long racks stacked with fishing rods. The counter was glass-fronted, featuring dozens of little compartments filled with flies and lures.

“Bernie!” Esme yelled, hurrying up to the counter. “Bernie!”

"I'm coming, I'm coming!" a cranky voice called from the storeroom. "Hold your horses."

A portly young man wheeled into the room, moving his wheelchair with strong flicks of his sturdy wrists. Bernie's black hair was streaked with copper where the sun had bleached it, sprawling in unkempt curls from under his floppy hat. His cheeks were ruddy, nose peeling, and a scruffy beard clung to his round cheeks.

"Esme, right?" he said. "You look just like the old lady."

"Sorry for barging in," said Esme. "Grammy always talked about you. It feels like I know you, even though we've barely met."

Bernie laughed. "I know the feeling." He raised his bushy eyebrows. "You're not here for fishing tackle, are you?"

"No." Esme smiled. "I think you have something for me."

Bernie nodded solemnly. "Yes, I sure do." He went to the low counter and opened the old-fashioned cash register, then fished around in the piles of pennies, dimes and nickels.

"Here," he grunted. "This's for you."

He gave her a heavy brass key, one that looked exactly like it would fit in the chest's padlock.

"Yes!" Esme squealed. "Thank you."

She whirled around to look for Joe, but her happy squeal died on her lips. Joe stood by the door, his phone pressed to his ear. He held out a hand to her, telling her to wait.

Something popped inside Esme and made her shrink. She lowered her hands, still clutching the key.

"Give me ten, Bob. Sorry about that. Thanks so much. See you." Joe lowered his phone and grabbed Esme's hand. "We've got to go, babe. They need me urgently on a call about this meeting."

"Okay," Esme whispered.

Joe hurried down the street, still holding her hand. They were almost out of Mermaid Cove when she said, "Bernie had the key."

"Mm, I saw," said Joe, too absorbed in his phone to notice the way Esme was looking at him.

Chapter Twelve

Esme hefted the stone elephant with a grunt. It was beautifully carved; now that she'd spent a few minutes cleaning it up, she could see the careful, intricate swirls that patterned its back and rump. When she slid it into place as a bookend on the shelf, it looked perfect next to a tiny cactus with a single red flower and an action figure of Tardin of Merrabor.

She stepped back, hands on her hips, and a small smile flickered back into place on her face. With three library shelves now tidy, a warm sense of satisfaction bloomed in her chest, almost erasing the sting of pain that still sat there. Almost.

The library door opened. "Esme?"

She didn't look around. "Don't you have a meeting, Joe?"

Joe sauntered in. "It's done now. The next one is tomorrow." He cleared his throat. "Listen, I'm sorry I didn't pay much attention back at the tackle store. I'm under a lot of pressure with this."

"I know." Esme sighed, allowing guilt to mingle with the pain in her chest. She turned the stone elephant slightly so that the light struck it at a better angle.

"Did it fit?" Joe asked.

Esme turned to him. "Did what fit?"

"The key," said Joe. He gestured at the chest, standing on the small table in one of the bay windows.

"I don't know. I hadn't tried it yet." She'd been so upset when she rushed into the library that she'd just left the chest where it was and turned her energy to tidying up.

Joe ventured a smile. "Do you want to try?"

Esme pressed a hand into her pocket and felt the small, sharp shape of the key. "If you don't mind."

"Not at all, Es. Come on. Let's put this morning behind us," said Joe. "Let's try."

Esme wasn't sure that putting it behind them was that simple, but she followed Joe over to the bay window anyway and pulled the key from her pocket. It slipped easily into the lock, and she twisted it. Smoothly oiled, the lock popped effortlessly open.

"Yeah." Joe grinned. "It worked!"

His enthusiasm felt a little false, but Esme appreciated it anyway. She unhooked the lock, set it aside, and gripped the lid. "You ready?"

Joe nodded. "Let's see what's inside."

Esme hesitated. What would it be? A more formal will stating what she'd been left? A pack of bills? More than a small part of her thought she'd flip the lid open and look down into a stack of gold coins.

She took a deep breath and opened the lid.

"Wait, what?" Joe frowned.

Esme blinked, trying to comprehend what she saw. There were no documents inside, nor any money or gold. Instead, there was a wooden board about halfway up, with a little silk bag resting on it.

"What is that?" Joe asked.

Esme picked up the bag and opened it, turning it upside down over the chest. A pile of colorful disks tumbled out.

"Are those... checkers?" said Joe.

Esme pushed the disks aside. "No." She laughed. "They're pucks. It's like a miniature game of shuffleboard."

"Shuffleboard?" Joe picked up one of the pucks and smiled. "That brings back memories, huh?"

Esme returned the smile. "I still can't believe that you actually went to games night when James invited you."

Joe had been visiting a friend in Boston who happened to be Esme's best friend's brother. They'd planned to go out for drinks the night that Avery had invited James and his friend to the game night they hosted at the house that Avery, Esme and Jenny had shared. Esme hadn't thought much of the shy stranger at first, but then they'd been paired for a game of Pictionary, and it had been as though they could read each other's minds.

"Remember how we crushed them in Thirty Seconds?" Joe smirked.

"It was like telepathy." Esme laughed. "But you could always absolutely destroy me in shuffleboard."

"I guess this is the next part of your grandma's game." Joe raised an eyebrow. "So, do you think you can beat me this time?"

"You're out of practice, Joe. I think I can kick your butt!"

"Let's see about that," Joe teased, the old sparkle in his eye again.

The game was awkward to play on such a small surface, but Joe was still adept. Esme, however, had no such luck. Her pucks flew everywhere. One shot off the end of the chest and pinged off the vase of flowers on the small table. Another ricocheted on the edge and smacked her on the nose.

"Oww." Joe burst out laughing. "Are you okay?"

"This game is rigged," Esme grumbled, but she couldn't stop smiling.

"Sure, babe." Joe winked. "Keep telling yourself that." He flicked a puck expertly into the high-scoring zone at the end of the board.

Esme rolled her eyes in mock exasperation, but her heart felt like it had been filled up with sunshine. They hadn't laughed together like this in far too long. It was so easy, looking at the sparkle of his dark eyes as she lined up another puck, to remember why she had so easily fallen in love with him.

She shot the puck forward. It skidded over the high-scoring zone, bounced, shot back toward her, and ended up at the opposite end of the board from where she wanted it. "Oops."

"I have you now, love." Joe smirked. "I can't help but win."

"So arrogant," Esme teased.

Joe gave his puck an expert flick. It skidded onto the high-scoring zone, and with a soft click of wood, part of the board fell open like a trapdoor.

"Ooh." Esme leaned forward.

"What just happened?" Joe peered into the hole.

"The weight of the pucks must have triggered it." Esme laughed. "Where did Grammy find all this?"

"Who knows?" Joe ran his fingers around the hole. "She was a resourceful woman. Oh, there's something in here." He pulled out another tiny roll of parchment secured with a piece of purple ribbon.

"Another..." Esme stopped. "Another clue."

She looked at Joe's face, waiting for his outburst of annoyance that the treasure hunt wasn't over, but instead he was smiling. "Go on, honey. Open it. What does it say?"

Esme unrolled the note and read it out loud.

"*Well played, Joe!*

Where the meadow foams

look where heaven is."

Joe laughed. "She knew me better than I expected, huh?"

"She had a way of doing that."

"What do you think of the clue? Is there a meadow around here somewhere?"

Esme gazed out of the bay window. "No, but there is meadowfoam—a flower—and I know Grammy used to love planting them in the garden. I guess that's the next place where we should look." She wiped her hands on her pants. "If you have time. Otherwise, I'll just go."

"No." Joe put a hand over hers.

Esme raised her head. "Wh...what?"

"I was just thinking, Es." Joe cleared his throat. "It's Thursday night. Even if we caught a redeye tonight, there's no way I'd fit in a full workday tomorrow."

Esme's heart thudded. "Do you mean..."

"Maybe we should just stay until Sunday night," Joe suggested gently. "If we fly back on Sunday evening, I can be back in the office on Monday morning."

Three whole days to spend in Mermaid Cove. Esme's heart leaped at the thought.

"Would that suit you?" Joe asked. "Even if I hear from my clients today, I'm sure they won't want to meet before Monday."

"Joe, I'd love that. Thank you. I really would."

"I know." Joe leaned over and kissed her forehead. "But only until Sunday, okay, honey? I really can't stretch it any longer than that."

"I know," said Esme hastily. "I understand. It's fine."

"Good." Joe smiled. "Now I have to get back to work, so let's look through the garden in the morning. Okay?"

"Okay."

She watched him leave the room, the piece of paper still clutched in her hand. Three more days.

Then she would be going back to the apartment and the silence.

Esme climbed the staircase slowly, juggling a laden plate in one hand and clutching a glass of soda in the other. This spare bedroom had always been Isabel's favorite. Grammy used to call it the Heidi room; it was tiny and tucked away at the back of the house, on the same level as the attic, with a spiraling wooden staircase that led up to it. As little girls, Esme and her sisters had thought the staircase was romantic. Esme still thought so, although its impracticalities were becoming more obvious with a plate and glass in her hands.

She was slightly breathless when she reached the top. The door was arched and smaller than usual, and she knocked on it with her elbow. "Izzy? It's me."

There was a beat of silence. "Esme?" said Isabel.

"Yeah, I just brought you some dinner."

Footsteps thumped on the floor, and Isabel pulled the door open. She wore an oversized black tee shirt, featuring an extravagant piece of artwork that depicted a violin melting into a thunderstorm, and her hair was down in a soft, comfortable braid that made her look younger. It was startling to see her without her dark makeup.

"Aw, Es, you didn't have to." Isabel took the plate, piled high with Lance's signature lasagna. "Wow, that smells good."

"It was weird not to see you at dinner," said Esme gently. "Are you okay?"

Isabel stared at her for a second, then sighed and stepped back. "You'd better come in."

Esme followed her into the room, which hadn't changed since the last time she'd been here as a teenager. The black ceiling was covered in glow-in-the-dark stars. A painting of a wolf howling at a crescent moon hung on one wall; the tiny window was hidden behind navy curtains, and a single bed was pushed up against one corner, its covers all silver and navy, moon and stars. Isabel set the plate down on the nightstand and perched on the bed. Esme flopped into a big black beanbag in the corner.

"Sorry for not coming down." Isabel sighed. "I wasn't up to Mom. I'm leaving soon and I just thought she was going to try to fit in one last lecture or something."

"I get it," said Esme.

"You always do." Isabel picked up the fork lying on the plate and speared a piece of lasagna. "Oh, wow," she groaned with her mouth full. "Dad's cooking never changes."

"I know. The ultimate comfort food, right?" Esme laughed. "Looks like you could use a little more comfort food." She poked Isabel in the leg with her toe.

"Hey!" Isabel protested. "Are you body-shaming me?"

"Not at all. You look great, Iz. Seriously."

"Thanks. I have to, you know? Thousands of people see me under spotlights every night when we're on tour."

Esme tilted her head to one side. "It's hard work, huh? I never know where you get your energy from. You're always bouncing around like crazy on the videos."

Isabel's laugh was flat and empty. "It's getting harder to do that lately."

"How so?"

"Oh, you know." Isabel waved a hand. "Just a little tired, I guess. My passion will come back."

Esme said nothing, listening.

After a few more bites of lasagna, Isabel's jaw tightened. "Okay, so maybe I don't know if it'll come back."

"I'm sorry, Izzy. That's got to be hard. You've always loved the band so much."

"It's been my life for nearly seven years," said Isabel. "My whole life. I just write and play music, Es. Okay, I know I'm just a bass player and writer, but the band has always felt like my found family... until recently. I don't know. It all changed when Sean left. I know there were all these rumors about how we were together and stuff, but it wasn't like that. He was a big brother to me... a friend and mentor. He was the one who made sure the other guys didn't take advantage of me."

Isabel brushed a hand over her cheeks. "The guys look up to me now, so that's fine, but I guess it all just feels empty. I haven't written a song in months. It's more than just Sean, too. The last couple of years, well, I'm not sure if I was staying for the music or just because it felt like I belonged with the band."

"Maybe there are other places you could belong, too," said Esme gently.

"It feels insane even admitting it, but that's what I'm hoping." Isabel shrugged. "I guess that's why I came to Grammy's will reading. I was going to do the funeral and then bounce, and when I missed it, I thought I'd just walk by the place where they scattered her ashes and say goodbye. But I decided to stay for the reading." She let out a shuddering sigh. "Maybe because I thought it might tell me what to do next. Give me a new direction."

"Maybe it will," said Esme. "Did you open your riddle yet?"

Isabel shook her head. "What use would it be? I've got to play a show on Saturday. I can't stay much longer... I'll have to come back after the tour. Maybe I'll have forgotten about this craziness by then." Her eyes were desperate. "Maybe I'll be happy to have my life back."

"Grammy always told me that there are more forks in the road than we know about. We just have to be willing sometimes to pick up our machetes, cut through some jungle and see where the trail takes us."

Isabel laughed. "Yeah, that sounds like Grammy. I just don't know which part of the jungle I should go into, you know?"

"I hear you." Esme leaned against the wall. "You know what I wish?"

"What?"

"I wish we could all stay just a little bit longer. Do you remember what it used to be like on vacations here, all of us together?"

Isabel smiled. "Do I remember? Those were the happiest days of my life. I know Mom and Grammy were at it sometimes, but usually, even Mom loved those days, even if she wouldn't admit it. Bonfire nights and ice cream in the village and watching Grandpa teach Dad to surf and—" Isabel's voice choked up suddenly, and she stopped.

"I was thinking," said Esme, "if we all stayed for just a little longer, maybe we'd begin to remember. Maybe everything would get better then."

Isabel looked away with a harsh, barking laugh. "Oh, Es. I love you, but that's never going to happen."

Esme's heart stung. "Why not?"

"It's just not." Isabel put down her plate abruptly, like her appetite was gone.

"Our family was awesome once. We could laugh and play together. It was the kind of family that dreams are made of. Who's to say it can't be like that again?"

"Okay, sure, it was great back then." Isabel shook her head. "I'm not denying it. But there's a very good reason it'll never be the same, Esme, and you know it."

"What?"

Isabel met her eyes, pressing her lips together in an unhappy line. Tears glimmered in her lower eyelids.

"Our family worked for one reason," she said, husky with the coming tears. "Grammy. She was the glue that held us all together. She was the only magic we had. Now she's gone, and it's never coming back."

The words slammed into Esme's heart like an axe into the trunk of an old tree. Silence settled over the sisters, thick and heavy.

Chapter Thirteen

"Whoa," said Joe. "How are we going to find anything in this mess?"

The morning light was crisply golden; Joe had wanted to get started early, so he had time to help Esme before his first online meeting of the day. The salty tang of the sea mingled with the heady perfume of the flowers that spilled all over this part of the garden.

Esme remembered Grammy saying once that she wanted the garden to feel like Minotaur's labyrinth, which was why she'd had her landscapers arrange it in a maze of interesting sections, each walled off with tall hedges. This was the entrance to the main part of the garden—a vast lawn where Esme and her sisters had spent countless hours playing—and already Esme was starting to think that the rest had become more labyrinthine than even Grammy had intended.

She remembered this as a cute little section with the wrought-iron gate in one corner and rosebushes bordering the stepping-stones that formed a path to the archway leading to the lawn. Instead, she and Joe were looking into a jungle. The stepping-stones were almost invisible under the sprawling mass of blue beach asters.

The jasmine that climbed the archway had gone rogue, spreading its fingers into the unkempt bush of hedges. The rosebushes—all different colors—were wild explosions of blossoms and thorns, and the birdbath was bone dry, filled with leaves, and almost suffocating under the blue rose.

"She really let the place go in the last few years, huh?" Joe brushed his fingertips over the surface of a deep red rose. "I don't remember the gardens looking like this when we came here for the first time."

"I think it started when we all quit coming here on vacation." Esme wrapped her arms around herself. "I guess she was also just getting old."

"That makes sense. Still sad to see it like this, though," said Joe. "Where did you say you thought the clue would be? Was it here?"

Esme looked around. A few patches of common meadowfoam, bright against the asters, were scattered here and there. "I guess it could be, but I know Grammy had a wildflower garden on the other side of the lawn where there was a lot of meadowfoam."

"I think we'll need a machete to get there," said Joe.

Esme laughed. "Let's start here, I guess."

"It's going to take forever to sift through this mess." Joe frowned. "I'll be right back."

He turned and walked away.

"Joe!" Esme's heart sank. Had her husband already given up?

"Wait here," Joe called over his shoulder.

He returned a few minutes later, and he was grinning, carrying an armful of gardening tools: shovels, pruning shears, and a rake. He dumped them on the path at Esme's feet with a clatter.

"I haven't done much of the gardening thing," he admitted, "but I saw Ronald using these on Mom and

Dad's garden, so I thought we could use them and do a little cleaning up while we're at it."

Esme stared at him. "You're sure?"

"Of course. It's pointless trying to search through that chaos without doing at least a little tidying up," said Joe, "and it's a shame to see it like this."

Esme wasn't sure where this sudden burst of motivation had come from, but she wasn't complaining, either. She grabbed a shovel. "Let's get to work."

Within minutes, Esme had to roll up her sleeves to the elbows. Sweat trickled down the backs of her legs and into her sneakers as she bent over a rosebush, hacking back the overgrown stems and trimming it into shape. Joe was on the other side, wielding pruning shears as he tidied up the hedge.

"We're making surprisingly good progress." Esme straightened up from the first rosebush and tossed the extra sprigs onto a wheelbarrow she'd gotten from the garden shed.

"There are so many plants here," said Joe. "All we need to do is trim it back a bit."

The sun climbed higher in the sky, and Joe began to hum to himself. The sweet music of her husband's happiness made Esme feel as though she would never need to stop, like she could go on forever; it nourished her.

"Hey, honey, check this out," Joe called in excitement.

Esme lowered her shears and joined him by the hedge. Joe pointed to a tiny nest hidden deep among the twigs. It was inexpressibly neat, the little sticks woven tightly together, and contained four blue eggs no larger than Joe's thumbnail.

"Aww, they're so precious," said Esme.

"I wonder what kind of bird they came from," said Joe.

"Take a picture," Esme suggested. "Maybe we can look it up later."

She held the twigs aside carefully as Joe snapped a photo on his phone, then carefully let them shift back into place without disturbing the eggs.

"That was so cool," said Esme. "Like finding hidden treasure."

"Right?" Joe smiled. "Maybe we could have a nice backyard one day, too, when we buy a house."

House. Esme's heart flipped in her chest, and she gazed into Joe's eyes, trying to decide what he meant. A house with a backyard was something that only people with kids needed, wasn't it? Did it mean he'd changed his mind just like she'd changed hers?

He looked away, hands on his hips, and surveyed the small space. "Now isn't that better?"

Esme gazed at Joe for a long few seconds—the sheen of sweat on his neck, the dirt on his fingernails, the glow of satisfaction on his face—before she could tear her eyes away and look at their handiwork.

The wheelbarrow was piled high with discarded foliage. Each rosebush was neatly shaped, standing in proud rows on either side of the clean stepping-stones, the blue asters pushed back so that they grew in neat profusion around the stones.

There was still a wilderness about the place, in the meadowfoam that grew among the asters and the tangle of jasmine that spilled fragrantly over the archway, but it looked like a place that somebody loved now.

"There," Joe said, satisfied.

A bright, flashing bluebird fluttered down from the sky and landed on the edge of the newly filled birdbath. It chirped, hopped back and forth once or twice, then plunged into the water and bathed ecstatically, splashing a little cloud of spray into the air.

"It's perfect," said Esme, smiling.

Joe checked his watch. "Oh, wow, I need to hurry. Do you want to have a quick look around for the clue before I go?"

"Sure," said Esme. "Let's look around in the meadowfoam. I'll keep searching while you work, too."

They spread out, poking through the delicate white-and-yellow flowers, and it was only a few minutes before Esme's foot bumped against something that clinked like pottery. She pulled the meadowfoam aside. A pretty pottery mermaid lay among the flowers, completely out of place, her whimsical smile directed at the sky.

Esme crouched down and lifted the mermaid. "Joe, look at this."

Joe hurried over, and Esme turned the mermaid over to show Joe the bottom of her tail. A plastic pouch was firmly glued to the pottery.

"What's in it?" said Esme.

Joe pried it open with a thumbnail. "It's a note, but it's sealed."

He handed it to Esme. It was a smaller version of the envelope that the first riddle had come in; also heavy parchment, slightly stained by the weather, and sealed with a heavy glob of red wax. Grammy's fountain pen had been at work on the front, too.

Give this to Brodie Chandler in the village.

"Who's that?" asked Joe.

Esme shrugged. "I have no idea. If Grammy mentioned him, I don't remember."

"Well, I guess they have to be on Google Maps. Or on Facebook," said Joe. He checked his watch again. "I'm sorry, babe. I've really got to get to my meeting."

"That's okay. We found the note, didn't we? And look at what we accomplished."

But Joe didn't look. He was already rushing across the newly cleared stepping-stones, pulling his phone from his pocket. When he brushed against the wheelbarrow, several clippings fell out onto the freshly swept stones, and he didn't notice.

Esme popped her head around the study door. Half of her expected to see Grammy at the desk, crashing away at her keyboard, tongue sticking out of the corner of her mouth, peering through her half-moon glasses as she invented some captivating tale that readers would fall in love with. Instead, the woman sitting in the chair was Louise.

Esme was struck by how much like Grammy she looked. Of course, there was none of the crazy hair or cute glasses: Louise wore contact lenses and pulled her brunette hair back into a ferociously tight ponytail. But something about the slow expansion of Louise's proportions made her look more and more like Grammy every day. Esme liked it, although she was sure Louise hated it. It made her more cuddly.

"Lou?" she said.

Louise looked up.

"Are you in a meeting?" Esme asked.

"I wish." Louise snapped the laptop shut. "I couldn't get any flights back because of some storm over the city and my client demands to meet in person. I'll only get to talk to them tomorrow or Monday."

"Can I bother you with something?"

Louise sighed. "Of course, Es. Anything for my big sis. What do you need?"

Esme took a seat in the squashy armchair opposite the desk. "So, Joe and I found the next clue in Grammy's riddle."

"Oh, nice. I meant to ask how that was going," said Louise. "I thought of opening mine over the weekend, but I got a flight back for tomorrow morning. It'll have to wait until work is a little less crazy."

"I hear you," said Esme.

"So what was the clue?"

"A name. Brodie Chandler. I thought you might know who it is, since you've got such a great memory. Apparently he's in the village."

"Brodie Chandler." Louise leaned back in her chair and pressed her fingertips together. "Brodie Chandler."

"Ring any bells?" Esme asked.

Louise pursed her lips, then shook her head. "Sorry. I feel like I should know the name, but I can't put a face to it. Grammy might have mentioned him a few times, but I have no idea who he is. Maybe you could ask Mom."

Esme grimaced. "I don't know. Mom is really not into the whole idea."

"I have no idea why." Louise laughed. "You know Mom would crack a riddle like this in minutes."

"I know. She's so creative. She gave me really great ideas when I tried to get her to help me yesterday, but you know how she is. She's still mad."

"She's wasting time being mad." Louise shrugged. "It is what it is. I mean, it's a bit crazy, but that's how Grammy was. You'd think she'd know that by now."

"Yeah." Esme exhaled. "Can I tell you something?"

"Of course, sis."

"I'm not at all ready to leave." Esme reached out and brushed her fingertips over the desk. "I know that when I go, I'll probably never see this place again."

Louise's eyes softened. "Why do you say that?"

"Because you know that the likeliest person to inherit this house is Mom." Esme's shoulders sagged.

"And you also know exactly what Mom will do with the house when she gets it."

Louise sighed. "Actually... I do know. Exactly."

Esme frowned. "What do you mean?"

"I overheard Mom talking to Dad last night," Louise admitted. "Maybe I shouldn't have been listening, but I did."

Esme leaned forward. "What did she say?"

Louise bit her lip. "She told Dad that as soon as 'that idiot lawyer' gets disbarred, she'll get 'a real lawyer' to take over Grammy's estate. She'll get Grammy's will overturned. And then Grammy's property will be divided as if she didn't have a will. Since Mom is Grammy's closest surviving relative..."

"She'll get the lion's share," Esme finished. "Including the house."

"And she'll sell it to Preston in seconds," Louise agreed.

Esme covered her face with her hands, helpless against the anger washing over her. "How could she?"

"Preston's offering millions. The numbers do make sense," Louise said.

"Who cares about the numbers? Look at this place, Lou! It's filled with magic. We can't let that be taken away."

"We might not have a choice if poor old Reginald gets disbarred."

"Do you..." Esme stopped. "Do you think Mom's the one who lodged the complaint against him, the one I told you about?"

Louise smoothed her hands over her closed laptop like she longed to open it again and retreat into the world of numbers.

"I don't," she said finally. "I know Mom can be difficult, but she's not like that, Es. She wouldn't tank Reginald's entire career just because she wants the house. Mom's not grabbing for money, either. She just wants all this to go away."

"You're right there. Mom was never into Grammy's fortune. I always got the feeling she thought it was dirty money," said Esme.

Louise nodded. "Weird, but true. Who do you think *did* lodge the complaint, though? It definitely wasn't one of us."

"It was Preston. I'm sure of it. He used to be in love with Grammy, you know, years ago when they were in high school, and he has... some kind of weird complex about it."

"You think?" Louise lifted her eyebrows.

"That's what Corrie says. She thinks he's something like a stalker," said Esme, "and now he'll do anything to get his hands on the house. Since he knows Mom will sell it to him..."

"Disbarring the lawyer is in his best interests," Louise finished. "Oh, no. I hope poor Reginald will be okay."

"We can always find out." Esme picked up her cellphone and dialed Reginald's number.

He answered after a few rings. "Hello, Esme."

"Hi, Reginald. You're here with my sister, Louise, and I." Esme put the phone on speaker. "We were worried about you after that complaint. Somebody mentioned you could be disbarred."

"Disbarred?" Reginald exhaled. "No, no. That's almost impossible."

"How so?" Louise asked.

"I haven't committed fraud," said Reginald bluntly. "I would have to commit a serious offense for disbarment to be on the table. At the worst, I might face sanctions."

"Okay." Esme sighed. "Any progress on the complaint?"

"Nothing yet. As it stands now, I'm still handling Alicia's estate." That hint of fire crept into Reginald's tone again. "I plan to continue doing so."

"Good. I hope you do," said Esme. "Good luck."

She hung up and gazed across the desk at Louise.

"So his career should survive," Louise murmured, "but if he's sanctioned, he may lose control of the estate. Then Mom would get her hands on the house. And she'd sell it to Preston."

"Exactly." Esme ran her hands over the arms of her chair. "I'm not ready to see it go," she admitted. "Not any more than I was ready to see Grammy go."

Louise stared down at the surface of the desk, her eyes distant. "Me neither."

Chapter Fourteen

In the end, it was Corrie who had the answers.

Esme and Joe walked to the village in the blistering heat after his meeting. No one else in the family had any idea who Brodie Chandler was, but Esme was pretty sure Corrie would know.

"Corrie knows everyone," she told Joe as they trudged along the street, watching as a flock of tourists headed for the beach.

Corrie did, but not in the way Esme had expected. She frowned down at the note, her free hand stroking the cat that lay curled in her lap.

"Chandler," she muttered. "Chandler. Oh, you mean the guy that Alicia named her pirate captain after?"

"Chandler Bloodblade had a real-life inspiration?"

Corrie chuckled. "Try the docks. They'll be your best bet."

The docks were on the other side of town, which, given the size of Mermaid Cove, meant a fifteen-minute walk along a sandy path past empty, dormant beach homes, their shades drawn, until their owners could fill them up with laughter when summer was at its height.

A row of wooden berths stretched out from the rocky shoreline that formed a curving arm around the beach, sheltering it from heavier waves. They were mismatched, all different lengths, all different kinds of wood, and the boats floating beside them were as eclectic as they were.

A gleaming yacht, sail furled, hung serenely secured by strong mooring lines, the glossy letters on its side spelling out *Serendipitous Pride*, beside a small fishing boat with peeling paint designating her *Anna*. The rest of the handful of vessels in the docks of Mermaid Cove ranged everywhere in between.

"So," said Esme, half-jokingly, "which of those boats looks like they belong to somebody called

Brodie Chandler who inspired my granny's pirate captain?"

Joe chuckled. "Well, given that your grandma was a millionaire, I think it's best we go talk to the captain of *Serendipitous Pride*."

He pointed as a tall man in a surprisingly formal button-up shirt and khaki shorts disembarked from the gleaming yacht and strolled along the docks.

"I'm not sure," Esme hedged.

"Worth a shot, right?"

Esme smiled, the tension between them dissolving as she remembered the way Joe had thrown himself into straightening out the garden that morning. "Yeah. Worth a shot."

They met the well-dressed man halfway along the docks. He almost brushed past until Joe raised a hand and said, "Excuse me?" in the polite yet commanding voice that Esme had heard him use over the phone.

The man stopped. "Do I know you?"

Esme's eye caught on a burly man tossing smelly fishing nets over the bows of *Anna*. He wore a squashed and misshapen sailor's hat; his beard looked unkempt, and the bottom of his pale, hairy belly protruded from under his faded polo shirt.

Joe smiled, ignoring the question. "We're looking for a Brodie Chandler."

The stranger huffed. "I don't know him."

A roar burst out from beside the scruffy *Anna*. Joe and the stranger wheeled around to stare at the hairy fisherman, who clutched his abundant belly, great ripples running through it as he laughed.

"Something funny?" the stranger demanded.

"Don't know Brodie Chandler?" The fisherman screamed with laughter. "Don't know *Brodie Chandler*. Well, I'll be."

The stranger flushed scarlet, turned and strode away.

Esme inched nearer to the fisherman, Joe close on her heels. "Excuse me," she said. "I take it you do know Brodie Chandler?"

"Oh, everybody knows him, miss," said the fisherman.

"Do you know where we can find him?" Joe asked.

"Yeah," said the fisherman. "Right behind you."

Esme realized that a shadow had been cast over her. She spun around and looked up into the face of Chandler Bloodblade, Terror of the Sunset Sea, the man who'd sunk a hundred Dread Ships in one night, the man who was rumored to speak the tongues of sharks and whales.

She blinked, and the illusion melted away, because except for the eyepatch, the peg leg and the eighteenth-century Caribbean pirate garb, the man towering in front of her was the spitting image of Grammy's colorful fictional character.

His hair was a wild, grizzled shock around his head; the beard unfurled down to his chest, windblown and curling with salt air. The sun and wind had etched deep lines into a face the same deep brown as the groaning, creaking wood of the ancient ships that had explored this very coastline centuries ago.

"B–Brodie Chandler?" Esme stammered.

The old sea captain's face unfurled into a smile. "That's me, young lady."

Esme cleared her throat. "My name is Esme Gordon, and this is my husband, Joe."

"Ah." Brodie's face softened. "Alicia sent you, didn't she?"

A knot formed in Esme's throat. "Yes."

"Ha." Brodie chuckled, a soft, rumbling sound. "Crazy old pistol. This way."

He turned around and stomped away, heavy boots thudding on the wood.

Esme stared at Joe. For a moment, she thought he'd turn back or tell her that this was madness. But he smiled, his eyes sparkling, and took hold of her hand. "Let's go!"

Esme laughed, and together, they went.

Brodie Chandler's boat was somewhere in between the snobby man's gleaming yacht and the small fishing boat.

Laughing Bella was an elderly speedboat whose engines still purred with comfortable power. Despite her age, her polished wooden gunwales gleamed in the sun as she skimmed across the flat sea, Brodie's hair streaming behind him as he steered her toward the tiny speck of an island on the horizon.

"Alicia said you'd come," he boomed. "I figured it wouldn't be long when I heard the old gal had been reunited with Rod at last."

Reunited. It was an interesting choice of words, and it made Esme wonder who Bella was—or had been.

"Did she tell you about the riddle?" Esme asked.

Brodie laughed. "She didn't tell me the answers, if that's what you're getting at."

Joe had an arm securely wrapped around Esme's shoulders. "I don't think either of us would dream of trying to cheat Alicia's riddle."

"We're having far too much fun solving it," said Esme.

Brodie's grin parted his beard in a flash of startling white. "All I know is that she told me you and your husband would be here soon after she died. She told me where to take you." He reached into his shirt pocket and pulled out a grubby scrap of paper folded into a neat square. "And to give you this."

As the boat neared the diminutive island, Esme gripped the paper tightly, nervous to unfold it in the blowing wind. The island was no bigger than Grammy's lawn. Limpid waters surrounded it, and it looked like the cartoon of a desert island: a little heap of sand topped by a palm tree, its fronds stirring gently in the breeze.

Brodie brought the boat to a sputtering halt. "That's as close as I can bring you," he said, "but the water'll only be waist deep when you hop out. I'll be waiting here for ye."

"Waist deep?" Joe removed his phone from his pocket.

Esme handed hers to Brodie. "Let's go."

She splashed into the water, grateful she'd chosen to wear shorts, and her toes sank immediately into silty sand. Cool water splashed over her bare tights, then soaked into her shorts. She laughed, and Joe stepped down beside her with a little more caution, grabbing her arm.

"I've never been this deep in the ocean before," he yelped.

Esme giggled. "You're fine, babe. I've seen you do laps in the pool at the gym."

"This—this isn't the gym," said Joe breathlessly. "What's that?" he shrieked.

"It's seaweed! It's only seaweed." Esme brushed it aside. "Don't worry. We're okay."

Joe clutched her hand tightly and Esme guided him to the shore of the strange little island. Soon the cool silt between her toes turned into sunbaked sand. She retrieved the paper from the pocket of her blouse and unfolded it while Joe breathlessly wrung out his shorts and tried to figure out where he was going to put his phone.

"Oh." Esme laughed. "Look, babe. It's a map."

It was beautifully drawn in bright watercolors, creased by folding, showing the tiny island with its palm tree. A sea serpent paddled through the waters on the island's north. *Here be dragons... if you will,* Grammy's calligraphy announced on the east of the island. Beside the palm tree, six boot prints led to the west, then ended in a bright red X.

Joe laughed. "X marks the spot, huh?"

Esme looked up at him, but his eyes shone. There was no mockery in his tone.

"It can only mean one thing, right?"

"Well, look at that guy." Joe gestured toward the boat and Brodie. "It's got to be buried treasure."

"Now you're starting to think like Grammy," Esme laughed.

"I'm starting to believe that that's not the worst thing." Joe took her hand. "Come on."

They ran barefoot like children across the warm sand to the palm tree, where Joe peered at the map again. "Six bootprints," he murmured.

"Six paces?" Esme suggested.

"It's got to be. But mine or yours?" Joe asked.

Esme bit her lip. "Grammy drew this map. I think she was probably the one who paced it out. She wore the same shoe size I do."

"Then let's try it."

Esme stood with her back to the tree and measured out six steps, heel to toe. Joe crouched in the sand at her feet, trailing his fingertips down the back of her damp leg in a way that made goosebumps scatter pleasurably across her entire torso. She tried to calm the wild thundering of her heart as he passed his fingers through the sand.

"There's something here," he said. "Something hard."

Esme fell to her knees, scooped her hands into shovels and pushed the sand away. Joe joined in. It was loose and soft, and in a matter of seconds, their hole was several inches deep.

"There it is," said Esme, touching a plastic corner of something sticking out through the sand. "Do you think that's just some litter or something?"

"I guess there's only one way to find out."

He was crouched on his knees across from her, beach sand dusting the fine dark hair of his calves and forearms, bare feet tucked underneath him. The sea breeze brushed his brown hair into rippling waves. A hint of suntan had crept across his nose and cheeks in the past few days, bringing out the freckles he hated and Esme loved, and his eyes were bright in a way she hadn't seen in what felt like forever. The sight made her heart soar.

Joe leaned forward, pressed his fingers into the damp, clumpy sand and pulled it aside. Esme joined in, and in a few seconds they had freed something small and oblong—something laminated.

Joe grabbed it by the corner and pulled it out. It was an envelope tucked into a sealed plastic pouch, and sure enough, Esme's name was written in flowing calligraphy across the front.

"Some treasure," said Esme.

"We don't know yet. Can I tear it open?"

Esme moved around to his side of the hole they'd dug, and she realized he hadn't gotten around to putting on his cologne. He smelled of sunshine and of Joe, her Joe, unadorned and perfect. "Sure," she said breathlessly, almost forgetting about the envelope altogether.

Joe grabbed the edge of the plastic pouch and pulled. It tore open easily, and he eagerly widened the hole, then fished out the envelope and handed it to her with a little flourish. Esme smiled as she thumbed the wax seal.

"What do you think it is, babe?" she asked. "A more formal will, maybe?"

"I don't know, but whatever it is, your grandma wanted you to have it."

It was true. Esme popped off the wax and slid the envelope open, then grabbed its contents and drew them into the light.

It wasn't an official document at all. Instead, one side was printed with a bright, colorful photograph, showing a table set for two on a wooden porch that overlooked the beach, the sunset brilliant on the waves. Esme flipped it over with her heart in her mouth.

Coral Kitchen, the fancy script across the top intoned.

"This voucher entitles Joe and Esme Gordon to a four-course meal of their choice," Esme read slowly.

Her gut knotted. She knew full well that Grammy hadn't left her a meal voucher for an inheritance. This scavenger hunt wasn't over yet, and she didn't know how Joe would feel about that. She raised her eyes slowly and froze when she saw the huge smile stretching across Joe's face.

"Oh, wow," he said, taking the voucher from her. "This looks amazing. Isn't Coral Kitchen the fancy place you were telling me about?"

"Yes, I've never eaten there. It's pricey and Grammy only ever took Grandpa. She said—" She swallowed. "She said it was their spot."

"Romantic," said Joe.

"It does look romantic."

Joe reached over to take her hand, and Esme felt her heart skip a beat. "Let's go, then."

Esme blinked. "R...really?"

"Of course, babe." He laughed. "I'm not going to turn down the opportunity to have a sumptuous dinner with my stunning wife, am I?"

Esme met his eyes. *Two days ago, you would have.* Maybe Grammy was right, she thought. Maybe Mermaid Cove had magic in it after all.

Chapter Fifteen

THE LAST BITE OF the chiffon cake melted on Esme's tongue. She had no idea how it was possible for a single mouthful to be both rich and light, but this cake nailed it. Closing her eyes, she let out a tiny moan of pure delight.

Joe's hand tightened over hers. "This stuff is amazing."

Esme opened her eyes, smiling at the expression on Joe's face. "You've got a little—" She hesitated. "Here."

She picked up her napkin and leaned over the table to dab a few pale crumbs from his upper lip. Joe's eyes found hers, and she froze for a moment, their faces only inches apart.

Coral Kitchen was once a grand colonial home overlooking the little bay on the other side of

Mermaid Cove's docks. Tucked deeply among a thicket of box elders and Californian buckeyes, the restaurant's seating filled the ground floor and spilled onto a sweeping porch that ended where the beach sand began.

Grammy's voucher had caused the waiter to smile knowingly and lead them to a VIP area on the balcony of what had once been the master bedroom.

Now, Joe and Esme were alone, and when she looked past him at the silent ocean, it was possible to imagine that they were the only people in the world. Soft jazz filled the evening air. The balcony was strewn with fairy lights, and citronella candles fluttered on their table.

Joe was the one who leaned closer. Their lips met, and a familiar flutter ran through Esme's chest.

A delicate cough broke them apart much too quickly. Esme sagged in her chair, disappointed, as their waiter drifted through the open doors, carrying a tray with timeless elegance.

"May I bring you anything else?" he enquired. "More drinks, perhaps? Another dessert?"

"No, thank you. I don't think I can eat another thing." She smiled. "I've never had such excellent Californian clam chowder before. That sourdough!"

"It was amazing," Joe agreed, "but my favorite was definitely the starter. What was it called again?"

The waiter smiled. "Oyster Kirkpatrick, sir. I will pass on your compliments to the chef."

"Please do," said Joe. "This place is a gem. We'll definitely be back."

We will? Esme's heart leaped, but she quieted it. Joe couldn't mean that. In a few days they were going back to Chicago, and she'd never see Mermaid Cove again.

"It has been a pleasure to serve such a lovely couple." The waiter reached for something on his tray. "I have one last item for you, left by the lady who purchased the voucher."

"Oh." Joe laughed. "I was having such a great time, I almost forgot this was part of the treasure hunt."

"You must think this is all kinds of nuts."

The waiter shook his head. "I served Alicia regularly, and she was always a delight." He held out a familiar parchment envelope sealed with wax. "She told me that when I give this to you, to tell you this: it's the last clue. This is the one that will lead you to the answers you're looking for."

"Thank you," Esme murmured.

She took the parchment and held it for a few moments as the waiter retreated.

"Are you going to open it?" Joe asked gently.

Esme forced a smile. "Yes."

"You look upset, honey." Joe squeezed her hand. "What is it?"

"It's just—" Esme's eyes welled. "These might be the last of Grammy's words that I'll ever read."

"That's not true." Joe smiled. "You only have to open one of her books to hear her voice."

"Thank you, baby. I needed to hear that." Esme broke the wax with a fingernail and slipped the parchment out of the envelope.

Built in 1829

hidden among the stones you'll find

what once was mine.

I ran out of rhyme

but know this:

the stone which the builders rejected

the same is become the hiding place.

Joe frowned. "Okay, I'm lost."

"1829." Esme frowned. "Where have I seen that number recently?"

Joe snapped his fingers. "Above the door of your grandma's mansion."

"Of course! The mansion was built in 1829."

"Hidden among the stones. The original structure was river rock, right?" said Joe.

"Yes. It used to be a farmhouse. There's been a lot of additions, but the back portion—where the kitchen is—that's all still the original house. Do you think we have to search there?"

"She must have hidden it somewhere in the wall," said Joe. "That's all I can think."

Esme frowned. "What could she have hidden in a wall?"

"Paperwork," said Joe promptly, "transferring ownership to you. It could be anything. Maybe a vehicle."

"Grammy drove a Zimmer Golden Spirit," Esme remembered.

"I know." Joe melted into the table. "Baby, if you inherit that thing, I'll love you forever."

"Hey!" Esme gave him a playful poke to the shoulder. "We're married, remember? You're supposed to love me forever anyway."

Joe's laughter filled the night, and Esme joined in. It was pure and effortless and harmonious, and if this was the only gift Grammy had left her, it was enough.

Joe was on his hands and knees, head buried in the kitchen cabinet. There was a loud clatter, and several pots fell onto the kitchen floor.

Esme looked up from where she crouched barefoot on the counter, trying not to break anything as she ran her hands over the ancient stonework by the window. "You okay, honey?"

"Fine," Joe panted. He sat back, hair awry and draped with cobwebs. "I could use a coffee. How long have we been looking?"

Esme glanced at the old clock on the wall, its pendulum swinging in quiet rhythm. It clashed dreadfully with the rest of the kitchen, she thought. It would suit the Heidi room so much better. "It's nearly ten."

"Coffee?" Joe suggested.

"Definitely coffee." Esme flicked on the machine. "I don't understand. We've searched every visible stone inside and out of the house, and there's no loose mortar, no clues, nothing."

"I hear you," said Joe. He prodded the stove with a finger. "Do you think it's behind something?"

"Why would Grammy put it behind something built-in?" Esme wondered.

Joe laughed. "Because she was Grammy. She did what she wanted."

"She sure did. Let's try."

An hour later, their coffees had grown cold on the kitchen table, and they were both covered in dust, sweat and spiderwebs. They'd moved the stove and dishwasher, unpacked the cabinets on the wall, and even unscrewed the ugly clock.

“Oh, come *on*,” Joe groaned as Esme ran her hands over the wall and shook her head.

“There’s just nothing here.” Esme dragged her forearm over her sweaty brow.

Joe picked up the clock from the kitchen table and grabbed a screwdriver. “I’d better put this back.”

“No, don’t. It doesn’t belong here. It was making my eye twitch.” Esme flopped into a chair and slurped her cold coffee. “I don’t get it, Joe. Why would Grammy make this impossible?” A knot formed in her throat. “Maybe I’m not as smart as she thought I was.”

“Oh, Essie, no. That’s garbage. We’re going to find it. We just need to look at the letter again.” He pulled it out of his pocket. “You knew her so well—you knew how she used to think.”

“I’ve read it a thousand times,” she said.

“Read it again.” Joe spread it out on the table. “I know you can do this.”

She met his eyes and smiled. If *Joe* believed she could, then she could. She smoothed down the page and reread the words.

Built in 1829

hidden among the stones you'll find
what once was mine.
I ran out of rhyme
but know this:
the stone which the builders rejected
the same is become the hiding place.

"The stone which the builders rejected," Esme echoed.

"Is there a heap of rubble out there in the garden somewhere?" Joe suggested. "Maybe a stone wall they built out there from the river rocks that weren't good enough for the house?"

"Not that I know of." Esme sighed. "And we've already inspected every imperfect rock we found in this wall."

"What was she talking about, then?"

Esme said again. "The stone which the builders rejected, the same is become the hiding place. It sounds so familiar."

"It does, come to think of it, but something's out of place."

"The stone which the builders rejected, the same is become—" Esme stopped. "Joe, that's it."

Joe straightened. "That's what?"

"I know what it means." Esme scrambled to her feet and yanked open a series of kitchen drawers.

"Grammy kept rocks in there?" Joe said.

"No, but she used to keep a Bible stashed in every room, in case of emergencies, she always said." Esme yanked open a drawer full of dishcloths. "Here."

She pulled out a leather-bound King James Version with gorgeous gold-edged pages. She had to look up the words in her Bible app to find the verse, but in a few seconds, she'd paged to Matthew 21:42.

"'Jesus saith unto them, Did ye never read in the scriptures, The stone which the builders rejected, the same is become the head of the corner: this is the Lord's doing, and it is marvelous in our eyes?'" she read.

"The head of the corner?" said Joe.

"The cornerstone. It's the cornerstone, Joe."

Joe clapped her on the back. "I knew you'd get it, Essie."

"Come on." Esme grabbed his hand. "We have to find it."

They raced outside into the overgrown jungle that had once been Grandpa's vegetable garden. Radishes, beans and a sprawling patch of potatoes, all mingled with sprigs of wildflowers and weeds, straggled against the old river rock.

"Ouch!" Joe yelped, wading through a pumpkin patch near the back door.

"You okay?" Esme called.

"Yeah, I just hit my shin on something." Joe crouched down. "Oh! Honey, I've got it."

Esme hurried to his side. They pushed aside the spiky stems and fat blooms of the pumpkins and uncovered the worn cornerstone that had weathered every crisis California could throw at it for nearly two hundred years. The inscription was barely visible: *Rogers, 1829,* the letters rough-hewn and ugly, chopped into the stone not by a skilled mason but by a proud farmer whose family had a place to call home.

"There." Joe pointed with a trembling finger. "There's something underneath."

Esme saw it, too, the corner of something plastic, like the one they'd uncovered on the island. She gently pried it from the deep earth under the stone. It was a sealed plastic sleeve, containing two items this time: another parchment envelope, and a plain, ugly manila one, large enough to hold documents.

Esme's breath caught. "You were right."

"Open it," Joe urged.

Esme's hands were shaking too much, so Joe took the plastic from her and tried to tear it, but this was made of even sterner stuff than the sleeve on the island. Knees wobbling, Esme followed Joe into the kitchen. He found a pair of scissors in the drawer she'd just rummaged through.

"Not here," Esme quavered. "The study."

Joe took her hand. "Okay."

They sat facing each other over the desk in Grammy's study, the desk where she'd created the world and characters that had enraptured so many people of so many different ages, and Joe cut open the sleeve with a few snips of the scissors.

"Which one first?"

"Wait." Esme put a hand on his. "Joe..."

He put down the sleeve and wrapped her hand in both of his own. "I know, honey. It's the last one."

"It's not that. Before we open it, I just wanted to thank you."

"For what?"

"For these last few days." Esme smiled. "I could never have done this without you. I've loved every minute we've spent together, and it just reminded me that, well, you're my best friend. I'm so happy I married you." She searched Joe's eyes. "I'm so in love with you."

Joe's gaze softened. "I'm in love with you too, Essie. This has been really great."

"It's been more than just fun playing and problem-solving with you," Esme went on. "It's shown me we make a great team."

"I agree," said Joe.

Did she dare to say it? Esme searched his eyes and saw nothing but love and gentleness there. It was now or never. If she didn't say the words now—if she didn't voice the quiet conviction that had been growing inside her ever since her return to Mermaid Cove, perhaps even before that—she would never have the courage to say them.

"Es? What is it?"

"It's just—I think you and I can do anything." She swallowed. "I think we could even be great parents one day."

Joe's face froze, and Esme knew instantly she'd made a terrible mistake.

"Parents?" he demanded, snatching back his hands as though she'd burned him. "Esme, are you thinking of—of having kids?"

Esme opened her mouth to deny it but couldn't. It would be the most atrocious lie she'd ever uttered if she said that she wasn't thinking of it. She had been thinking of little else since that morning in Mermaid Cove when they'd watched the children on their bikes racing down to the cool sea.

Joe sagged in his chair. "You never said you wanted kids before. We've never even talked about it. I thought—" He stopped. "I thought you never wanted any."

"Maybe I didn't, when we got married." Esme's words came out in a rush. "But Joe, haven't you ever looked at a parent with a baby in the park or in the mall and wondered what that would be like? What it would be like to hold a little human, the perfect blend between yourself and the person you love the most in the entire world?"

She stopped. Joe was shaking his head side to side, his eyes wide, leaning away from her as she spoke.

"Why have you never told me about this before?" he demanded.

Tears filled Esme's eyes. "Because I wasn't sure, honey."

"And you're sure now?"

"Yes."

"Why?" Joe demanded.

Esme swallowed her tears. "Because it feels like I've gotten to know you and fall in love with you all over again since we came to Mermaid Cove, and now I know I want your children. Our children. I'm not sure why we never talked about it."

Joe pressed his hands into his hair. "Esme, do you hear what you're saying right now?"

"Is it that ridiculous, Joe?" said Esme, her voice cracking.

"Yes." Joe waved his arms. "What makes you think that I have time for kids?"

His words slapped her in the face, and Esme fell back in her chair. "Why couldn't you make time for kids?"

"Because I have a career, Esme! I need to work my way up in this company, or—"

"Why?" Esme shot back. "We have everything we need. Why do you have to keep driving and driving for the next promotion?"

Joe stared at her. "You know why."

"For more money?" Esme threw up her hands. "I never wanted more money, Joe. I wanted you."

The color drained from Joe's face. "Apparently, you want kids." He pushed back his chair and got up. "Something I never knew."

"Joe—" Esme began.

He raised a hand, silencing her, and strode out of the room.

"Joe!" Esme called.

The door slammed behind him, a sound that echoed through the fabric of her being.

Chapter Sixteen

For a few long moments, Esme sat motionless at Grammy's desk, her hands buried in her hair. She was aware of her heart thudding heavily in her neck and wrists, of her shuddering breaths as she fought to hold back the tears.

Waves of pain washed over her body. Joe had been so alight, so happy just a few minutes ago. Having fun, collaborating, problem solving. She knew he would be an excellent father.

If only he wanted the same thing that she did.

The weight of her sadness threatened to crush her, and Esme dragged herself to her feet. She plodded to the nearest bookshelf, seeking the quiet company of those fictional worlds, and took down one of Grammy's treasures: the hardcover edition of her newest book. It had come out just a few weeks ago; the paperback was not yet published. When Esme opened it, the spine creaked with newness, and the fresh smell of ink and paper filled her senses.

She held the book closer to her face and inhaled. New book smells always reminded her of Grammy. When she was a kid, Gwen used to leave her with Grammy most summers, at Esme's request. Grammy would take her along as she toured the country for book signings and interviews. Wherever they went, there was fun and laughter, and the smell of new books.

That was all over now. Having a husband who always worked and a career that wasn't her whole life, what did Esme have left? Long, silent, empty days.

It was at a book signing that Grammy had first met Joe. Joe and Esme had been dating for a few months, and he'd come to Boston for a visit over the summer. It had meant everything to Esme that Joe would use some of his seldom-touched time off to be with her. It had been the first time that Esme thought Joe could really be the one.

Coincidentally, during the week Joe spent in Boston, Grammy held a book signing at Harvard

Book Store. Clutching the author copy of the latest *Tales of Otherworld* novel that Grammy had sent her in the mail in one hand, Joe's fingers loosely entwined in the other, Esme led him to the charming bookstore to meet the most influential person in her life.

He'd raised his eyebrows at the book's cover—a splashy, stylized drawing of a unicorn-riding, sword-wielding knight galloping across ocean waves—and raised them even further at the sight of Grammy, whose hair was green and purple that summer.

When they reached the front of the line, Grammy hugged Esme until her ribs creaked. Then she smiled at Joe in a way that she'd never smiled at any of Esme's boyfriends before.

"Smart as a whip, you," she said. "You'll do fine with my little fairy."

When Joe smiled back, enraptured, Esme felt herself falling in love.

Now, she blinked and closed the book, then returned it to its place on the shelf. The warmth of the memory drained as though blown away by a storm wind at sea. Maybe Grammy was wrong about Joe, after all.

It was surely possible for even Grammy to be wrong about things.

Esme stumbled back to the desk and sank down in front of the two envelopes, still in their plastic sleeves, the scissors lying beside them. She needed answers now more than ever. Maybe they lay in what Grammy had left her.

She opened the parchment envelope first and read the last message from her grandmother.

Fairy,

You have always been a great hero in my eyes. May this castle be worthy of the queen that you are.

Never give up. Rejoice always. Pray incessantly. When you love, love with the ferocity of dragonfire, just as I have loved and will always love you.

Grammy.

Esme pressed the letter to her chest for several long moments, allowing the tears to roll freely down her cheeks. She swallowed hard, set the letter aside, and reached for the larger envelope. It was thick with documents, and when Esme opened it, the first was an official letter. She skimmed over the letterhead and her eye caught on a paragraph halfway down.

... hereby confirm that I leave the house and grounds at number 10, Summer Avenue, Mermaid Cove, CA, to Esme Gordon...

Esme blinked. Surely this couldn't be right. This had to be a crazy mistake. With shaking fingers, she grabbed the other document.

There was no mistake. The document was the title deeds of the mansion and its land, and it was in Esme's name.

Grammy had left her the house.

Esme staggered into the kitchen, hugging the documents close to her chest. It felt as though her feet didn't quite touch the floor. The beautiful flagstone floor of the house she loved.

The floor of *her house.*

"Esme? What are you doing? You look like you've seen a ghost."

Esme looked up. Gwen stood at the kitchen counter, busily chopping vegetables.

"What's that?" Gwen asked.

"I finished the riddle."

"What?"

"I know what Grammy left me." Esme's voice was quiet, choked with emotion.

Gwen stared at her. "*What*?"

"The house. Grammy left me the house."

She held out the papers to her mother, and Gwen snatched them up. Her eyes scanned over the papers, and she stood motionless.

"Is it real, Mom?" Esme wasn't sure this could be happening.

Gwen slowly nodded.

"Yes. Yes, it's real, Esme. This is ironclad. There's no doubting the paperwork." She thrust the papers back into Esme's hands. "The house is yours."

"Oh, Mom." Tears spilled over Esme's cheeks.

"Best call Preston quickly. Before he changes his mind about the excellent offer that's on the table."

Esme gave her a long look. As if she could ever sell the house.

As if she had no choice but to go back to Chicago.

A wave of reality washed over her and she didn't know what to do. So she fled.

Chapter Seventeen

THE DOCUMENT IN ESME Gordon's hand was only a few pages long, but as she held it against her chest, it carried the weight of her world.

As her toes sank into the warm sand, Esme strolled along the beach with an overwhelming heaviness in her heart. If the weather dared to match her mood, it would have been stormy, with thunder and lightning. Instead, the evening was as picture-perfect as Southern California could be.

Sunset painted the sky in improbable shades of deep pink, fading to royal purple. The sun shimmered on the watery horizon, a double coin of burnished gold, reflected in the gentle ripple of the waves.

With the sea and sky both engulfed in such dramatic color, it was easy to imagine that Esme had escaped to a different world, somewhere fantastical and worthy of grand adventure.

Esme closed her eyes and tried to imagine it, but the weight of the document she held in her hand kept drawing her back to this life, this world that was so bitterly void of magic.

Sighing, Esme stopped and turned her back on the sea to gaze at the mansion where it towered over its overgrown grounds and the unkempt footpath leading to the beach. The golden evening light bathed its façade in brilliant color, lighting up every window, every roof tile, every streak of peeling paint.

For an instant, Esme allowed the thought to swell in her heart: that this place was hers, that it could be home. The idea rose in her like a giant bubble, and she crushed it. This could never happen, she knew. To dream would be to have her heart broken beyond repair.

The hum of a Rolls-Royce engine caught her ear. Esme froze and looked up as the gleaming silver vehicle bumped to a halt on the grass with an eerie similarity to the previous time she'd been walking alone on the beach. It blocked her path back to the house, and she felt suddenly cornered and alone.

She pushed the thought away as Preston doddered out of the car and limped toward her, swinging his cane. She had nothing to fear from this old man.

"Good evening, Esme," he called cheerfully.

She had to clear her throat a few times before she could speak. Suddenly, she wished she'd locked the deeds in Grammy's study before coming outside.

"Hello, Preston."

He walked toward her, smiling, his eyes unusually warm and bright. "Your mother told me the excellent news. You're a very lucky young lady—and you're about to be a very rich one."

"Excuse me?" Esme's senses were on alert.

Preston pulled a piece of paper from his pocket. "This would have been more dramatic with a check, but who uses them these days?" He handed it to her. "Here's my offer on the house."

Esme unfolded the paper and stared at it. The number was so large that she could barely comprehend more than a jumble of zeroes. The thought of having that in her bank account seemed unreal, ludicrous, and unnecessary.

She looked up at Preston and imagined bulldozers flattening the study where Grammy made magic.

"No, thank you," she said politely, handing it back.

Something flashed in Preston's eyes. "I beg your pardon?"

"It's a very generous offer," said Esme, "but I don't want to sell the house right now. Thank you very much."

Preston's eyes narrowed, but he quickly replaced anger with a benevolent smile. "I'm not sure you understand, my dear. You are young, after all. The house market doesn't stay stable, you know. An offer like this might never come again."

"I'm still deciding if I'm going to sell the house at all," Esme said defiantly, although she knew it was likely. What else could she do with it?

Preston laughed. "Oh, I see. Your sentiment is clouding your rationality. Well, allow me to make this very simple for you." He smiled. "You should sell the house to me right now. You'll be millions richer,

Esme. In fact, if you invest this wisely, you'll never have to work again in your life."

Esme shook her head. "No, actually, I understand just fine, and I'm not interested in selling right now."

Preston took a step nearer, his grip tightening on his cane. "You're being a fool. You should sell it."

Sudden anger flashed through Esme's gut. She met the old man's eyes and straightened her back.

"No," she said.

Preston sneered. "Stop being ridiculous." He waved the piece of paper. "I'll add another million."

"No, Preston," she said firmly.

"No one else will ever give you this price."

"I don't care." Esme made no attempt to rein in her fury. "And I'm not the fool, you are. You weren't good enough for Grammy, and you're not good enough for her memory, either."

Preston reeled.

"If I do sell the house, I'll sell it to someone who appreciated her, who appreciates it. Not to you. It won't be knocked down for some fancy development. Now leave me alone."

Preston stepped nearer, his sneer widening into a grimace of fury. "Now listen here, you silly little girl," he snarled, "that house will be mine, or—"

"Hey!" a voice thundered. "You!"

Esme and Preston both looked around. Even in her anger, her breath caught at the sight of Joe striding purposely towards her. He wore a white linen button-up shirt with one button more than usual undone, and it was loose enough that the ocean breeze pressed it against the sculpted curves of his torso. He wore those same ugly swimming trunks—horribly mismatched with his shirt, but the only shorts he owned—and no shoes. The wind sculpted his hair as he approached them, hands clenched by his sides, eyes ablaze.

"Oh," Preston sneered. "The husband. Finally. Someone to reason with." He held out the paper. "I've given your wife an excellent offer on this place, and—"

Esme wrapped her arms around herself, ready to be told how wrong she was.

Joe slapped his hand aside. "And she has rejected it. Now leave."

Preston blinked. "What?"

Esme was almost as surprised as Preston.

"You heard me, and you heard her," Joe snapped. "That house and these grounds belong to my wife, and if she doesn't want to sell them to you, then they'll never belong to you. I think she made herself quite clear. You should leave."

"Read the number, and you'll realize how foolish—"

"Call my wife another name, and you'll regret it."

Esme's jaw dropped. She'd never heard her trust-fund-baby husband use that tone before, much less seen real danger in his eyes. It made her heart race, but not with fear.

Her Joe was standing up for her, and it thrilled her.

Preston's voice was low. "You're making a mistake."

"No," said Joe, "actually, this time, I know I'm not. Now please get off my wife's property. You're trespassing."

They stared at each other a few seconds longer. Then Preston spun on his heel and stalked back to his car.

"Joe!" Esme said.

Joe turned to her, the fire leaving his eyes.

"How did you know?"

"Gwen told me. I think she called Preston, too." Joe bit his lip. "So… you inherited the house."

A sharp ache rose in Esme's chest as their fight returned to her memory. She looked away.

Joe exhaled, thrust his hands into his pockets, and stared down at the sand for a few seconds.

"Esme, I don't know how to tell you how sorry I am."

His words caught her off guard. She took a step back. "What?"

"I know." Joe rubbed the back of his neck. "It hurts that you're so surprised to hear me apologize, but I understand it. I haven't been the husband that I should have been." He finally looked into her eyes. "That I want to be."

Esme didn't know where this was going. She stayed silent, listening warily.

"What you said in the study earlier." Joe swallowed. "About not wanting more money… but wanting me. Is it still true?"

Esme allowed her hands to fall to her sides with a rustle of paper. "Of course it's true, Joe. Otherwise I wouldn't have turned down Preston's offer."

He searched her eyes, and the silence hung.

"We're so privileged already," said Esme. "We have everything we need. If I wanted more, I guess I'd put more effort into my career." Admitting it lifted a weight from her heart. "Why would I want to have more stuff if you were never home? It would be pointless."

Joe crossed his arms tightly over his chest, as if trying to hold himself together. "You say it like it's obvious, but the way I grew up, it never was."

Esme thought of Joe's parents' home. The penthouse apartments in more than one city, the bulletproof retirement plan, the clever investments, the ferociously guarded trust funds. The way that his parents always sat on opposite ends of the couch, an icy space yawning between them. His father's wandering eye. His mother's Botox-tight lips.

"My parents were terrified I'd be spoiled," said Joe. "You know how Dad made all his own money with the company? Well, he's always expected me to do the same thing."

"The pressure that he places on you is insane," Esme agreed.

"Yeah." Joe sighed. "Truth is, Essie, I don't really want more, either. The thought of that promotion and having to spend *more* time at the office makes me sick to my stomach. You're right. We have what we need." His throat tightened. "I have *you*. There's nothing more that I want."

Esme swallowed. "Nothing more?"

"Okay, no. Maybe one thing more." Joe held out his hand.

Esme took it.

"You're not the only one who's been thinking of starting a family lately."

Esme's heart thudded. "I'm not?"

"No, baby, not at all. I've been watching all those parents in the park and at the mall and walking past the street from the corner office window, too." Joe's lip quivered. "My only consolation was that you didn't seem to want kids, so I could stay quiet about it without disappointing anyone."

"Why would you stay quiet about it?"

"Because the truth is, I don't know if I'd be a good father." Joe wiped his eyes. "My dad gave me everything, but he wasn't the kind of father I needed. More than anything, if I have kids someday, I want to be the dad they need."

"Oh, Joe." Esme clutched his hand tightly. "You would be an amazing dad."

Joe bit his lip. "These past few days have taught me that, like you said, there's nothing we can't do together." His tone turned gentler. "*We* would be good parents together, you and I."

Happy tears stung Esme's eyes. "I love you, Joe."

"I love you too, baby. Can you forgive me?"

"I already have."

He held out his arms, and she pressed herself into his embrace, into his scent, the strength of his body against hers, the feel of his arms around her, the texture of his skin against her cheek. They held one another for several long moments, trembling, and in that moment Esme realized Grammy was right after all: that magic is wherever you look for it.

When they stepped back, Joe's eyes were damp. He laughed faintly. "I guess we're going to have to give up the fancy apartment, huh? We'll need somewhere with a backyard to raise the kids."

Raise the kids. The words buoyed Esme's soul, giving her the courage to say, "Well, about that... This is a pretty big backyard."

Joe gazed at the beach and garden surrounding them.

His silence made her heart swoop.

"I mean, it's all ours. Ours to sell, if not to Preston." She smiled, her sadness about the house ebbing in the face of her joy about their future. "We can raise our kids anywhere we want. We can get a home with a big backyard, everything we want."

Joe stared from the house to Esme and back again. Then he reached out and took her hand and clasped it tightly, his grip trembling but resolute.

"What about right here?" he said.

Esme's heart pounded, the weight of hope almost too much to bear. "Wh–what do you mean?"

"What other place would be better for children to grow up?" Joe indicated the house, the ocean, and the small town in the distance. "This place is magical. Who in their right mind would ever let it go?"

"What are you talking about, baby? What about your job?"

"I can work it out." Joe smiled. "We can work it out. If we can figure out Grammy's riddles, we can figure out anything."

Esme's heart took wing and soared in the last glowing rays of the sunset.

"Anything," she said softly.

He pulled her closer, and their kiss was a homecoming, crisp with salty tears, fierce with passion, filled with hope.

Chapter Eighteen

Gwen eyed Esme suspiciously over the plate of pasta. It was hardly the type of food Esme craved in midsummer at the beach, but Gwen hated seafood and salads. Now, Esme tried to avoid her mother's stare and shoveled a forkful of lasagna into her mouth instead.

Gwen took a long sip of her red wine and set down the glass. "All right," she said. "Spit it out."

Everyone at the table looked up. Louise and Isabel were long gone, but Margot, Gwen, Lance, Joe, and Esme still sat in the kitchen for dinner.

"What do you mean?" Joe asked.

"Don't give me that," said Gwen. "You and Esme have been exchanging secret looks ever since we sat down for this meal. Esme, just tell everyone what you told me earlier."

The spark in her eye gave Esme hope that, someday, when she had bigger news, Gwen would be happy about it, too.

She looked over at Joe. "We might as well, right?"

Joe nodded. "Go ahead."

"Go ahead with what?" asked Margot.

Esme got to her feet. "Everyone," she said dramatically, "I have an announcement to make."

Lance looked up. "That sounds serious."

"It's serious, but it's also wonderful." Esme took a deep breath, and the love in Joe's eyes gave her courage. "Joe and I solved Grammy's riddle. I know what she left me."

Gwen's expression darkened.

"She left me the house," Esme announced.

Margot spat her wine. The red splatter sprayed against Lance's shirt. He didn't notice; he was too busy gaping open-mouthed at Esme.

Gwen closed her eyes for a few seconds, shaking her head.

"It's true," said Joe. "Alicia left her the house and land."

"Oh my goodness, Es, this is amazing," Margot gushed. "It's so perfect. You've always loved this house more than anyone else, maybe even more than Grammy did. Look at how nice it looks since you've started fixing it up. You're the perfect person to inherit it!"

"Thanks, Margie," Esme managed.

"Congratulations, honey," said Lance.

"Thank you," said Joe.

"What are you going to do with it?" Margot asked. "You're not going to sell it, are you?"

"No," said Esme. "No, we're not." She smiled at Joe. "Joe and I talked, and we decided that since he can actually do most of his job online and if the company he works for agrees to let him work remotely, we're going to move here."

Every drop of color had drained from Gwen's face; she was absolutely gray.

"Won't you both lose money that way?" asked Lance.

"A little, but that's where the second part of our plan comes in." Esme smiled. "We're going to turn a few rooms into vacation rentals. We're going to make the mansion a bed-and-breakfast."

"That is so perfect." Margot shrieked with delight. "Grammy would have loved for more people to enjoy the house."

"I thought so, too," said Esme.

"Aw, I'm so happy for you guys," said Margot. "This is amazing."

Esme stared at Gwen, and an awkward silence fell. Gwen's face was ashen. She pushed back her chair and rose to her feet. She neither stomped nor ran out of the kitchen, but her back was very straight, and her hands clenched by her sides.

"Mom?" Esme called.

Gwen didn't look back. She left the house quietly, not slamming the door, but it still clicked shut with a sound that shattered Esme's heart.

The mansion bathroom used to be horrifying. When Esme first set foot in it, it was decorated in awful pastel shades of pink and purple. The bath was half the size it could have been, and the ugly brown carpet clashed with the purple curtains.

Now, Esme sat on the edge of a gorgeous, massive bathtub against a window of one-way glass overlooking the bay. But her attention wasn't on the careful coordination of cream, white, and lilac in the room. Instead, she tried not to stare at the tiny plastic object, the size and shape of a digital thermometer, lying next to the basin.

Esme got up and checked her phone. One more minute.

She paced the bathroom. It was hard to believe that it had been just a few months since she and Joe had packed up everything in their Chicago apartment and left it behind for good. Mermaid Cove fit her like a glove; it had wrapped her in its embrace as snugly as though she'd never been away.

The timer on her phone beeped. Esme dropped it from trembling hands and had to get on her hands and knees to fish it out from under the chic little bathroom cabinet she'd restored. She shakily stopped the timer, shoved the phone into her pocket, and picked up the little plastic item.

She forced herself not to look until she pushed open the bathroom door and stepped into their bedroom.

Joe sat on the edge of their bed, the one with the new white covers that matched the curtains. He looked up, his eyes huge, face pale.

"What does it say?" he said quietly.

"I can't bear to look." Esme turned the pregnancy test toward him so that he could see the result. "What does it say?"

Joe didn't answer, but his smile told her everything she needed to know.

Happiness exploded in her, and her heart soared. She dropped the test as her hands flew to her mouth.

"We're having a baby, honey." Joe burst out laughing, tears shimmering in his eyes. "We're having a baby."

Esme ran to him and jumped into his arms. He twirled her around like they were still in high school, their laughter filling the room. She wrapped her arms around his neck and kissed his face until she was out of breath, and they both flopped onto the edge of the bed, holding each other, laughing and crying.

"I can't believe it." Esme pulled back, wiping away her happy tears.

"Congratulations, baby." Joe cupped her face in both hands, eyes shining. "You're going to be an amazing mom."

"Thank you," Esme whispered. She picked up the test and gazed at the line that told her how much their lives were about to change. "I can't wait till the first trimester is over."

"Why's that?"

Esme looked up at him, smiling. "I can't wait to tell everyone."

Joe beamed. "Me neither."

She turned the test over in her fingers, thinking. "There's someone I'd like to tell first. Maybe even before this trimester is over, if it's okay with you."

Joe tilted his head. "Who's that?"

Esme met his eyes. "Isabel," she breathed.

Chapter Nineteen

Isabel

BACKSTAGE SMELLED LIKE MAKEUP, disinfectant, and sweat.

Isabel cradled her bass guitar to her chest, carefully caressing the instrument's well-tuned strings. She'd already performed the sound check with her band earlier that evening, and now the openers were nearly done, the crowd yelling with a fraction of the wild glee they'd show in a few minutes when Mad Kitten stepped onto the stage.

"Yeah!" The drummer bounced in place with his usual relentless energy, eyeing the drum set on the stage. "Let's rock this, you guys!"

Isabel didn't have her phone backstage. She'd never minded before, but now she felt a wave of longing sweep over her. She'd had to cut the call with Esme short.

Esme had sounded excited to tell her something, but she'd had to go before she could find out what it was. Now she'd likely only be able to call her sister again after her show tomorrow night.

She already knew Joe and Esme had moved to Mermaid Cove forever. What could be more exciting than that? But her sister's voice had bubbled with enthusiasm.

The other band members yelled their agreement with the drummer. Rodney, their lead singer, jumped up and down, loosening his shoulders. His rakish grin lit up the space.

"Ready to do this?" he asked.

"Yeah!" their keyboard artist and backup vocalist chimed in.

Rodney glanced at Isabel. "What about you, Iz?"

Isabel smiled. "Yep, totally ready."

Rodney frowned, but before he could say anything, the band who'd opened for them scampered offstage, sweaty and giddy with the opportunity to play before

Mad Kitten. They nearly fainted at the sight of Rodney. None noticed Isabel.

"Ladies and gentlemen," the host announced from the stage, "please welcome the band you've been waiting for... Mad Kitten!"

Rodney bounded onstage, and the crowd went ballistic.

Isabel closed her eyes. She thought of a house on the beach, the house Esme had inherited and was keeping, a mansion filled with artwork and books and so much love.

She thought of going back to Mermaid Cove.

"Come on, Iz," the drummer urged impatiently.

Isabel opened her eyes. It was the memory of that small town in California that gave her the strength to stride onto the stage.

For more sweet romance, surprise twists, and small-town charm, read Isabel's story in "*The New Promise*," Book Two in the Mermaid Cove Romance series.

The New Promise

A Mermaid Cove Romance
Book Two

Fame brought her everything she thought she wanted—so why does she feel so empty?

After years of sold-out concerts and chart-topping hits, Isabel Weston should be on top of the world. But behind the music and bright lights, loneliness and doubt haunt her. When her sister Esme invites her to Mermaid Cove for a much-needed escape, Isabel agrees to return to the one place where she once found refuge—her late grandmother's house.

Determined to unravel the inheritance riddle Grammy left her, she reconnects with her past, including Pietro Ortega, the loyal and kind-hearted son of the local café owner, whose warmth is impossible to resist. But as their bond deepens, so does the shadow of her old fears and a secret she's never shared.

Just when she begins to believe in second chances, a devastating storm threatens to destroy everything Pietro's family has built—and the fragile hope blossoming between them.

When the last clue leads to an extraordinary discovery, Isabel must decide: Will she step into the spotlight on her own terms and fight for the love she's always longed for? Or will fear keep her running?

Escape to Mermaid Cove in this heartwarming tale of love, family, and the courage to find your true voice. Perfect for fans of sweet romance, surprise twists, small-town charm, and finding home where you least expect it.

A Special Gift

If you enjoy sweet romance, please enjoy your copy of *Coffee and a Kiss.*

Download this light-hearted short read and sign up for Megan's newsletter to hear about new releases, featured authors, giveaways, and more.

You can find your copy at

https://dl.bookfunnel.com/aizhmi51ktat

Coffee and a Kiss

Can a sea change heal a broken heart?

Susan Maxwell's day just got worse. An unwelcome surprise awaits her when she arrives home from work.

Her sister, Allie, insists she comes to the coast to catch her breath and heal her heart. Arranging to meet at a coastal café, Susan's attention is captured by the café owner Tom, who extends kindness and a listening ear. But when Susan's ex arrives unexpectedly to win her back, misunderstandings force her to decide - will she follow her head or will she listen to her heart?

About Megan

Megan writes heartfelt clean romantic women's fiction set in picturesque small towns nestled near the coast.

With relatable characters, sweet romance, and a touch of mystery, her stories offer readers the perfect escape to worlds they wish they could call home.

If you love tales of love, resilience, and new beginnings, framed by sun, sea, and sand, Megan's books are your perfect companion.

Besides writing, Megan enjoys playing tennis and pickleball, beach walks with her dog, and keeping tabs on where her two daughters are in the world at any given moment!

Follow Megan on Amazon, Bookbub, Goodreads, Instagram, and Facebook.

More by Megan

Looking for another clean romance escape?
If you enjoyed this story and love heartwarming coastal romance with a touch of mystery, there's plenty more waiting for you!

Visit Megan's Amazon author page – https://www.amazon.com/Megan-Jacobs/e/B08PKBB2YM – and start reading today.

Island Whispers Romance series
After the Wave – Lantern Cove series
The Beach Hotel series
Love at the Beach Cottage series
Vacation in Paradise series
Thula Beach series
Secrets from Seaview Villa series

Island Escape series

Mystery at Blue Water Bay series

Return to Periwinkle Cove series

The Beach House (Clearwater Bay) series

Roses in the Sand—novella

Saving Candlelight Inn—novella

Holly's Christmas Secret—novella

Christmas at Candlelight Bay—novella

Printed in Dunstable, United Kingdom

66394062R00139